Wild Irish Rose

Joan Wolf

Wild Irish Rose
By Joan Wolf

Copyright 2021 by Joan Wolf
Cover Copyright 2021 by Ginny Glass and Untreed Reads Publishing
Cover Design by Ginny Glass

ISBN-13: 978-1-94913-591-6
Published by Untreed Reads, LLC
506 Kansas Street, San Francisco, CA 94107
www.untreedreads.com

Previously published in 1984, 2014.
Also available in ebook.

Printed in the United States of America.

Without limiting the rights under copyright reserved above, no part of this publication may be reproduced, stored in or introduced into a retrieval system, or transmitted, in any form, or by any means (electronic, mechanical, photocopying, recording, or otherwise), without the prior written permission of both the copyright owner and the above publisher of this book.

If you purchased this book without a cover, you should be aware that this book is stolen property. It was reported as "unsold and destroyed" to the publisher and neither the author nor the publisher has received any payment for the "stripped book."

The scanning, uploading, and distribution of this book via the Internet or via any other means without the permission of the publisher is illegal and punishable by law. Please purchase only authorized electronic editions, and do not participate in or encourage electronic piracy of copyrighted materials. Your support of the author's rights is appreciated.

Publisher's Note
This is a work of fiction. Names, characters, places, and incidents either are the product of the author's imagination or are used fictitiously, and any resemblance to actual persons, living or dead, business establishments, events, or locales is entirely coincidental.

The publisher does not have any control over and does not assume any responsibility for author or third-party websites or their content.

Also by Joan Wolf and Untreed Reads Publishing

A Difficult Truce
A Double Deception
A Fashionable Affair
A Kind of Honor
A London Season
Beloved Stranger
Born of the Sun
Change of Heart
Daughter of the Red Deer
Fool's Masquerade
Golden Girl
Highland Sunset
His Lordship's Mistress
Lord Richard's Daughter
Margarita and the Earl
Portrait of a Love
Someday Soon
Summer Storm
The American Duchess
The American Earl
The Arrangement
The Counterfeit Marriage
The Deception
The Edge of Light
The English Bride
The Gamble
The Guardian
The Heiress
The Horsemasters
The Master of Grex
The Portrait
The Pretenders
The Rebel and the Rose
The Rebellious Ward
The Reindeer Hunters
The Reluctant Earl
The Road to Avalon
The Scottish Lord

Chapter 1

Sara Underwood let herself into her mother's New York cooperative, went into the living room, kicked off her shoes, and subsided into a tapestry-upholstered chair. Flexing her feet, she let her gaze travel idly around the large, perfectly arranged room. Sara had never liked this apartment. The atmosphere, although perfectly comfortable and luxurious, was somehow cold and lonely, she thought. Sara sighed. She was tired from her day of shopping, lunching, and seeing people. Recently, it seemed as if she were always tired. Tired—and bored. The phone suddenly sounded, and after four rings Sara answered it. "Hello," she said impersonally into the receiver.

"Is that you, Sara?" a slightly nasal masculine voice asked.

"Hello, Rod," she answered, the faintest edge of boredom in her voice.

"Is your mother there?"

"No, she isn't home yet."

There was a silence fraught with frustration during which Sara stared at the ceiling. Then her current stepfather said, "Well, tell her I called, will you? Tell her I have to talk to her."

"All right, Rod. I'll tell her."

He made a noise as if he were going to say something more, but Sara said good-bye and hung up. She walked down the hall and into the gleaming modern kitchen to see what she could find to drink. The apartment was empty, as it was the servants' afternoon off.

Sara poured herself a glass of diet Pepsi and sat at the kitchen table. She noticed one of New York's tabloids lying on the table and picked it up to browse. The paper must belong to one of the servants, she thought. Her mother got only the *Times* and the *Wall Street Journal*.

As expected, one of the gossip columns featured a picture of her mother with a headline reading "OIL HEIRESS DUMPS NUMBER FOUR."

As Sara read the article, an expression of distaste slowly crept across her face. She put the paper down, rose, and went back into the living room, where she paced restlessly, moving from a priceless Chinese vase to a Watteau painting to an antique highboy and then back to the vase.

Finally Sara came to a halt at a window that overlooked the East River. Her gaze went beyond the traffic on the FDR Drive to the slow-moving barge making its way down the river, and her mind settled into a familiar groove. When I get married, I will never ever get a divorce. When I have children, no matter how busy I am, I will never ever leave them alone with the servants. When I ...

The phone rang again, interrupting the familiar litany.

Sara picked up the receiver. This time the call was for her. More plans, she thought moodily as she hung up. More appointments. More food she didn't want to eat, more people she didn't want to see.

She was poised over the phone, hesitating as to what to do next, when her mother came into the apartment. "Sara," the familiar silvery voice said from behind her. "Who was that, darling?"

The expression on Sara's face altered before she turned to face her mother. "That was Giancarlo," she said with indifference.

Lorraine Burnett smiled. "My, my, my. He's becoming very attentive, isn't he?" She waved a graceful hand. "Sit down, darling. We haven't had a real chat in ages."

Sara eyed the small, elegant figure of her mother as she sat once again in the ivory tapestry Queen Anne chair and folded her hands in her lap.

"So tell me everything, darling," her mother said encouragingly.

"Tell you what, Mother?"

A slight frown furrowed Lorraine's flawless forehead. "Tell me about Giancarlo, of course."

"What do you want to know?"

"I want to know what any mother would want to know. Good heavens, Sara! Is he serious?"

Sara shrugged. "I don't know. He's only pursuing me because I won't go to bed with him. I think he finds me a novelty."

Lorraine's eyes narrowed. "How clever of you, darling."

Sara's wide mouth turned down at the corners. "It's not cleverness, Mother; it's lack of interest. He is rather old."

"Old! He's not old. Giancarlo can't be more than thirty-five."

"Well, I'm twenty-three. To me that's old."

Sara realized too late that this was hardly a tactful statement. Lorraine was ten years older than Giancarlo, the Prince of Bolzano, and certainly did not like being regarded as old. The frown between her perfect brows deepened. "If I remember correctly," Lorraine said acidly, "you refused Jerry Hibbard because he was too young. And he's twenty-seven."

"He wasn't a serious person," Sara said defensively.

Lorraine cast her eyes upward in disbelief. "Not a serious person," she repeated ironically. "Really, Sara, you are the most difficult child ..." Lorraine launched into one of her favorite topics, and Sara sat stonily and listened. She had long since perfected the look of sulky insolence with which she effectively hid the depths of insecurity and guilt that her mother's words invariably evoked in a character that was not nearly as sophisticated as Sara liked to pretend.

"Rod called," she said when her mother finally stopped to catch her breath. "He wants you to call him back."

"Rod is a bastard," Lorraine said pleasantly, "and he can talk to my lawyer."

Sara had never particularly cared for Rod. She shrugged her slender shoulders and said indifferently, "Tell him that yourself, Mother. I'm not about to get into the middle of your quarrel."

Lorraine regarded her daughter with ill-concealed exasperation. "You're just like your father," she said for perhaps the thousandth time in Sara's memory. She did not mean it as a compliment, but Sara, who did not wish to be like Lorraine, was always secretly pleased when her mother spoke this way. She said nothing, however, and Lorraine's eyes narrowed slightly as she regarded her daughter's face. "Just like him," she repeated. "Obstinate and unreasonable. And you look more like him every day." Lorraine's voice was strangely abrupt—harsh, almost, not at all her usual sweet tone.

"Do I?" Sara's face retained its cool, indifferent mask.

Lorraine continued to look at her daughter, taking in the wide, sulky mouth, the straight hair the indescribable color of leaves in autumn, the darkly lashed golden eyes. On her first husband those eyes had been hawklike, arrogant, and dedicated. On her daughter they were most often disconcertingly aloof and ever-so-faintly bored. Lorraine felt a familiar wave of irritation sweep over her. "You've had everything a girl could want," she said impatiently. "Private schools, lessons in virtually every sport that exists, fabulous vacations, finishing school in Switzerland, a debutante season in New York. And are you happy? Are you satisfied? No." Lorraine pressed her lips together tightly. "You're just like your father. Nothing satisfied him either. He was only happy when he was racing cars at outrageous speeds somewhere or other in the world. And look what it got him—a grave at the age of twenty-nine."

"Is that why you divorced him, Mother?" Sara asked tentatively.

"Of course it was. What good to me was a husband who spent his whole life trying to kill himself?" Lorraine stood up abruptly. "I'm going out to dinner before the ballet tonight," she said. "I'd better start getting ready or I'll be late."

As she swept out of the room, Sara's mind settled into its habitual refrain: *When I get married, I will never ever get a divorce....*

*

All of Lorraine's previous divorces had proceeded relatively smoothly, but Rod was proving harder to dump than Lorraine had anticipated. He wanted a large cash bonus in order to bow out gracefully, and Lorraine was not inclined to give it to him. The divorce dragged on through the winter months. The papers loved it. They also jumped at Sara's friendship with the Prince of Bolzano and periodically announced an imminent marriage. Sara seriously considered the possibility of getting a job and moving into an apartment of her own. The only problem was that her very expensive and international education had given her virtually no marketable skills—and New York apartments were expensive.

In early April Sara came home after a Junior League lunch to find a strong-jawed, gray-haired man of about sixty-five pacing up and down her mother's living room, talking in a brusque, authoritative, uncompromising voice. Lorraine was seated in one of the Queen Anne wing chairs, looking very small and very fragile. It always astonished Sara—that air of fragility her mother projected—for Sara had never met anyone less fragile than Lorraine. At the moment, Lorraine looked decidedly unhappy and her large hazel eyes swung to Sara with unmistakable relief.

"Sara," she said. "Darling, look who's here."

"Hello, Grandpa," Sara said, walking across the floor to kiss her mother's father on the cheek. At five feet, seven inches, she was almost as tall as he was.

Hard gray eyes regarded her face and her purple skirt suit shrewdly. "You've turned into quite a beauty, Sara," he said, turning to Lorraine. "She looks just like Johnny."

"Yes," Lorraine said. "I know."

"But it sounds like she's got the brains of her mother." William Aronsen did not mean to be complimentary, and Lorraine's mouth tightened. "I want these newspaper stories stopped, Lorraine," her father warned. "I don't care what it takes to buy this bastard off, but I want the stories stopped. Do you hear me?"

Lorraine nodded her feathery blond head. "I hear you, Dad," she said faintly.

"And I want no more divorces." Mr. Aronsen's voice was heavy and threatening. "There's no law that says I have to leave you my money just because you're my only child."

"You wouldn't!" Lorraine stared at her father in horror.

"I would. And let me tell you now, Lori, I'm sick and tired of the mess you constantly make of your life. Your choice in men is nothing short of disastrous, and this last one is the worst of all. Christ! A golfer who has never finished in the top ten in any tournament he ever played in. And he's seven years younger than you, and a greedy bastard to boot."

Sara felt an unexpected flash of sympathy for her mother. She knew all too well how it felt to be on the receiving end of such a verbal assault.

"And you, miss," Aronsen said, suddenly turning to face his granddaughter. "What do you have to say for yourself?"

His harsh, accusatory voice made Sara's stomach tighten with nervousness, and she took refuge behind her usual mask. "Whatever do you mean, Grandpa?" she asked coolly.

"I mean it seems to me that you're about to go the same road as your mother. Who is this middle-aged Italian prince you've been making headlines with?"

"He's not middle-aged," Lorraine protested. "He's only thirty-five."

"He's too told for Sara," her father said uncompromisingly. "He's only a few years younger than the bum you're trying to dump." Lorraine winced visibly.

"The newspapers make the headlines," Sara said, "not me. I see the Prince of Bolzano socially, Grandpa. That's all."

Her grandfather looked her up and down. "Do you like New York, Sara?"

She took a deep breath before answering. "No. I don't." She did not look at her mother.

"Good. At least that shows a lick of sense—more than your mother ever showed, at any rate. Well, then, how about coming home to Kentucky with me?"

Sara's lips parted slightly. "With you, Grandpa?"

"That's what I said. You haven't visited the farm since you were a little girl."

Sara raised her brows. "I wasn't exactly deluged with invitations."

For the first time since she had come in, Sara saw her grandfather smile. "You're right. Maybe I've left you to your mother for too long. But you're my only grandchild and I hate to see you following in the same footsteps as your mother."

Sara would rather die than be like her mother, but loyalty kept her from saying so. "I'd like to go for a visit, Grandpa," she admitted. "It would be lovely to get into the country."

"Good. That's settled, then. I have some business to attend to while I'm here in New York, but it shouldn't take more than two or three days. You can come back to Canfield Farm with me then."

"Fine," Sara said eagerly.

Lorraine sat up in her chair. "Just how long is this visit to last, Dad?" she asked a little shrilly.

"For as long as Sara wants to stay."

Lorraine bit her lip and looked with stormy eyes at her only daughter.

Sara smiled at her mother with what she hoped was reassurance. "I would like to get out of New York for a while, Mother—for the summer, at least."

"Plenty of nice boys in Kentucky," William Aronsen grunted. "And no middle-aged Italian princes."

Sara grinned. "Thank God for that," she said, and they both laughed.

Chapter 2

Daniel Riordan whistled to his dogs to follow as he went down the road to the paddocks where the yearlings were kept. A middle-aged man with thinning hair and a weather-beaten face turned around as one of the German shepherds ran up beside him. The man was Henry Gordon, trainer for the Canfield Farm racing stable. "Daniel," he said to the young Irishman who was in charge of all the yearlings on the farm, "I wanted to talk over a few of these prospects with you before I leave for Maryland."

"Surely," Daniel said, nodding his shapely black head and leaning on the rail next to his boss. For the next half-hour the two men were absorbed in conversation about the slender-legged, good-looking young horses that were playing in the wide expanse of white-fenced paddocks. Then they turned away together and walked back along the road toward the barns.

"I understand Mr. Aronsen is bringing his granddaughter home with him," Henry said, seemingly at random, but his brown eyes darted a quick sideways look at Daniel.

"Oh?" the younger man said politely. "She hasn't been to visit before, has she?"

"Not since she was a kid. She lives in New York with her mother. According to Frances, she was running around with some middle-aged Italian prince and that's why the old man is dragging her back to Kentucky." Frances Smith was William Aronsen's secretary and the source of Henry's information.

"She sounds just like her mother," Daniel said.

"I'm afraid so. It's too bad—the old man deserves better. But the granddaughter is nothing but trouble."

Daniel stopped, and the dogs instantly circled around and came back to him. He looked up slightly at the taller, older man and said softly, "Is there any reason for this conversation, Henry?"

Henry Gordon stared into the blue eyes of his young assistant. When Daniel had first come to Canfield Farms, he had not had an easy time of it. He had the sort of good looks other men found hard to trust. During the four years he had worked at the farm, however, Henry had gained both respect and affection for the Irishman. So now he said bluntly, "Watch out for her, Daniel. She may decide you're the very thing to alleviate the boredom of the countryside."

Daniel didn't say anything, but slowly began to walk forward again. There was a thoughtful look on his deeply tanned face. Henry, who judged he had said quite enough, quickly changed the subject.

*

Sara arrived at Canfield Farm four days after Henry's conversation with Daniel, and at four o'clock, William Aronsen took her down to the barns to show her around. Since Henry Gordon was in Maryland for the Pimlico meeting, Aronsen asked Daniel to conduct the tour.

Daniel approached them as they stood in the sunlight outside one of the brood-mare barns. He wore a short-sleeved blue knit shirt, faded dungarees, and scarred and muddy tan work boots. His skin was very dark from the sun, his black hair cut short at the neck and sideburns. He greeted Canfield's owner courteously and nodded pleasantly to Sara. He then proceeded to take them around the barns and the paddocks.

Sara tried very hard not to stare at him. She listened to his soft voice, with its unmistakable Irish accent, and found her eyes returning yet again to his face.

"Would you be having any questions, Miss Underwood?" he asked. Sara, afraid he had caught her staring at him, felt a flash of embarrassment.

"What is your job here?" she asked, hoping her cool tone would disguise her interest in him.

"I work with the young foals and the yearlings," he answered courteously.

"What do you do with them?"

"We halter-break the foals and get them used to being handled. The yearlings we break to ride."

"It sounds fascinating," Sara said, and she meant it. But she was still embarrassed from having been caught staring and so refrained from looking at him.

"Daniel also rides jumpers in steeplechases," William Aronsen said. "When he can fit it into his schedule."

"I didn't know you had horses that jumped, Grandpa," she commented.

"Oh, they're not my horses. Daniel rides mainly for the Debretts down the road. They've raised jumpers for generations."

"I've never seen a steeplechase," Sara remarked.

"They're more popular in England and Ireland than they are here in the States, Miss," Daniel said softly.

"No money in jumpers," Aronsen said amiably.

"No." Daniel's voice was perfectly expressionless. "I'm afraid there isn't."

*

Daniel, by virtue of his rank as assistant trainer, had a small cottage to himself, but he usually ate with the men who lived in the dormitory near the barns. It was easier than doing his own cooking.

"I hear you met the granddaughter, Daniel," one of the grooms said as they began digging into their plates of pot roast.

"What's she like?" one of the others asked curiously.

"She's a lovely witch," Daniel answered readily. "Golden eyes, white skin, sulky-looking mouth."

The men watched him speculatively. "And what did she think of you?" one asked quizzically.

"Ah, Miss Sara Underwood will have no time for the likes of me," Daniel said good-naturedly. "I doubt she'd even know me again. She talked over my head the whole of the afternoon."

"If she's a female and if she has eyes, she'll know you again, Daniel," Red Markham, one of the older men said, and a chuckle of agreement ran around the table.

"Don't you be wishing me any trouble, Red," Daniel replied amiably. "Will someone please pass the butter?"

*

Canfield Farm sat on three thousand acres just outside of Lexington, Kentucky. In the immediate area resided some of the most famous families in American thoroughbred racing, and William Aronsen had his secretary call around the neighborhood and arrange a lawn party in order to introduce Sara.

"You don't have to put yourself out to entertain me, Grandpa," Sara said when she learned of his plans. "As a matter of fact, it's rather nice not having any social commitments."

"Nice for a day or two, maybe, but girls need company." Aronsen put down the spoon with which he was eating his fresh fruit cup and surveyed his granddaughter speculatively. She was wearing jeans and a green knit Izod shirt, and her hair was tied at the nape of her neck with a matching green ribbon. Except for a light touch of lipstick, her face looked innocent of makeup. "The Debretts have their grandson living with them," Aronsen said thoughtfully, looking at Sara's lovely face. "He's about your age, I think. I wouldn't be at all surprised if Ben leaves the place to B.J. and not to his son. Jimmy never was very interested in horses. It about broke Ben's heart, in fact. But B.J is a throwback to his grandpa."

"The Debretts," Sara said slowly. "Aren't they the family you said raised jumpers?"

"Yes," Aronsen said, pleased that she had remembered. "B.J.'s a great steeplechase rider. Won the Maryland Hunt Cup last year."

"Really?" Sara said with interest, even though she had never heard of the Maryland Hunt Cup. She looked around the patio where they were having breakfast. There were tubs of flowers everywhere. "It's so beautiful here, Grandpa. Why didn't I remember how beautiful it is?"

Aronsen grunted. "You were only a little girl the last time you were here, Sara. It was before you went off to boarding school."

"Yes, that's right." All Sara could recall from her last visit to Kentucky was that it was here her mother had told her she was divorcing her second husband. Sara had liked her stepfather, and the news had made her extremely unhappy. It had been hard to see the beauty of the farm through her own emotional turmoil, she decided now. She smiled at her grandfather a little wistfully and suddenly looked very young.

"What would you like to do today?" he asked.

"I'd like to see more of the farm."

Aronsen looked delighted. "Fine. I'll have Daniel take you in hand. You didn't get to see the stallions yesterday."

"It sounds wonderful, but I don't want to take Daniel away from his job," Sara said hesitantly.

"His job is to do as I tell him," Aronsen responded briskly. He rang a bell and a white-coated servant came out to the patio. "Have Daniel Riordan report to me, will you, Benjy?"

"Certainly, sir." The servant disappeared, and Aronsen poured himself a cup of coffee.

Sara buttered another hot roll, and her grandfather eyed her with satisfaction. "I'm glad to see you have a healthy appetite," he said approvingly. "You're so skinny, I thought you must be on a perpetual diet, like your mother."

Sara shook her head. "Mother's so small, she just can't eat that much," she said after swallowing her roll. "I have a lot more inches to fill up."

"Your father was tall."

"Yes, so I've heard."

"I guess you don't remember him much, do you, Sara? You were only two when your parents divorced."

Sara didn't reply, but the corners of her wide, full mouth turned down slightly. At that moment Daniel came out onto the terrace.

"You wanted me, Mr. Aronsen?" His blue eyes were on Sara's grandfather. Of her he took no apparent notice. He was simply here as an employee to see his employer, Sara thought.

"Yes, Daniel. I want you to show my granddaughter more of the farm this morning Take her all around; show her the stallions and the breeding operation."

"Yes, sir." His grave eyes then turned to Sara. "When would you like to begin, Miss Underwood?"

"I'll just wash my hands and then be right with you."

He nodded, and as Sara left the patio, she heard her grandfather say genially, "Sit down, Daniel, and have a cup of coffee with me."

*

It was ten minutes before Sara returned to the patio and found the two men chatting away comfortably. Daniel rose to his feet the minute he saw her. Her grandfather followed suit more slowly. "I'm ready," she said to Daniel.

"Fine, we'll be getting started, then." He nodded courteously to her grandfather and waited for Sara to precede him out the patio door.

"Would you like to ride around the farm?" he asked as they passed between the white columns of the porch and down the stairs.

"I had some riding lessons when I was a kid, but I haven't ridden since then. I doubt if I'd be up to the quality of your horses."

She smiled as she spoke, but his face remained grave. "We'll walk, then," he said. Two German shepherds that had been lying in the sun in front of the drive rose, shook themselves, and trotted over to walk beside Daniel. He looked at Sara out of the corner of his eyes. "If you don't like dogs, I'll send them home."

"You don't have to do that. They're beautiful." She stopped and held out her hand to be sniffed. "What are their names?"

"Fergus and Deirdre."

Sara patted an inquiring head. "I've never had a dog," she said enviously.

Daniel began to walk slowly, and the dogs and Sara followed. "Is that so, now?" he said. "I never remember not having a dog. Almost the first thing I did when I arrived in America was to get one."

"Why German shepherds?" Sara asked curiously.

He shrugged. He wore a light blue knit shirt similar to the one he had worn yesterday. He was a lightly built young man, but his arms were strongly muscled. Sara was suddenly embarrassed to be looking at his arms and resolutely directed her eyes forward.

"A fellow in the place where I was working told me about Fergus," he said. "He belonged to a family who wanted to get rid of him, and I said I'd take him." His voice altered subtly, became harder. "They'd after been abusing him, you see."

"Abusing him?" Sara looked at the beautiful, sleek head of the German shepherd walking at Daniel's heels. "How?"

"They beat him and locked him in a closet."

"My God." Sara was appalled. "Why on earth would someone be so cruel to an animal?"

He shrugged once again. "I don't know, but they fair made a wreck of Fergus."

"He seems fine now."

"Yes. It took some time, though."

"And Deirdre?"

"I bought Deirdre myself. She was the runt of the litter. She's come along well, too."

"She's gorgeous," said Sara.

She felt Daniel's eyes scan her face briefly but was too uncomfortable to return his look. She raised her chin slightly. "How long have you been in America, Daniel?" she asked in a voice that sounded haughtier than she realized.

"Five years, miss," he answered expressionlessly.

"And how long have you been at Canfield Farm?"

"Four years."

"Where in Ireland are you from?"

"Tipperary, miss."

"Do you have a lot of horses in Tipperary?"

He gave her another quick, slanting look and Sara felt herself flush. She hadn't meant to conduct an inquisition. "Ah, Tipperary, it's the Kentucky of Ireland. Tipperary and Kildare."

Sara bit her lip and walked on in silence. She still wanted to know more about him, but she didn't want to ask any further questions. After a few minutes he began to tell her about the stallions.

"We have thirty-two syndicated stallions standing here at Canfield," he said. His voice was detached and impersonal, and Sara glanced quickly at his profile.

"Thirty-two?" she echoed. "That seems like an awful lot."

"Canfield is one of the biggest breeding farms around. We have two Kentucky Derby winners and two Belmont Stakes winners standing here."

"What does that mean—standing here?"

A look of faint amusement crossed his face. "It means standing at stud. Their job is to impregnate mares. Among them they'll service over fifteen hundred mares this season."

Sara could feel a flush rising from her cheeks to her forehead. She felt both stupid and embarrassed. "Oh," she mumbled faintly, "I see."

He glanced at her again, and his amusement appeared to deepen. "Horses have very basic relationships," he said.

She looked at the toes of her Top-Siders as she walked beside him. "So it seems." She raised her head. Daniel was about three inches taller than she was in her flat shoes. "Do you breed only your own mares?" she asked with a good imitation of his detached tone of voice.

"No." As they walked along, he explained to her the process of syndicating a stallion, and Sara listened intently.

"My," she said when he had finished. "That basic relationship sure has a lot of complicated big business behind it."

He grinned. It was the first time she had seen him smile. And it was a smile worth waiting for, Sara thought, a little bedazzled and trying not to show it. "It surely does," he agreed. "It's a good thing the stallion doesn't know that. It might put him off his stroke." Sara laughed.

They spent the better part of the morning walking around the various paddocks, admiring the horses. Sara could not remember enjoying herself more. The sun was bright but not too hot. The grass was green and lush. White fences crisscrossed the gently rolling countryside, and glossy hides of brown, black, and chestnut shown in the rays of the spring sun. As they leaned on a fence and watched a group of brood mares with their long-legged foals, Sara looked up at Daniel. "They're so beautiful," she said simply. "They make me want to cry."

He looked back at her for a moment in silence. Her skin was flawless in the clear light, her lips curved with pleasure. Her well-marked brows and long lashes were naturally black, a startling contrast to the pale skin and lighter hair.

"Now, why should they make you want to cry?" he asked gently returning her gaze.

"I don't know. Beautiful things do, sometimes. Isn't it silly?"

"Do they now?"

"Yes." She smiled at him.

"I wouldn't say it's silly." He looked back at the horses. "You see the beauty. All some people see is money." He turned from the fence and headed back toward the road. Sara followed him. "Not that I have anything against money, mind," he remarked as they walked. Their strides suited together very well. "I wouldn't object to having a bit more of it myself."

"I know," Sara said. "Neither would I."

He raised an incredulous eyebrow. "Money of my own, I mean," Sara explained. "Money to do with as I want."

"And what do you want to do, Miss Sara Underwood?"

"I don't really know," Sara replied dismally. "I only know what I don't want to do. I'm in a terrible muddle, I'm afraid."

"Ah well," he said briskly, "it's only the rich who can afford the leisure time to be in a muddle. The rest of us have got to work."

He was right. Sara felt young, stupid, and worthless. She raised her chin and said dismissingly, "I suppose so." They walked back to the house in dead silence.

Chapter 3

"How did you enjoy your morning?" William Aronsen asked Sara at lunch. "Very much, Grandpa," she replied composedly. "I don't think I ever realized how beautiful horses are."

The old man looked gratified. "Do you ride?" he asked after a minute.

"I had some lessons when I was a kid. Mother was married to Derrick then and we were living in England. But I haven't ridden since then."

"I'll get Daniel to teach you," he said authoritatively. "He's an excellent rider and can teach you the proper seat."

Sara jumped at the chance to see more of Daniel. "I'd like that, Grandpa."

"Fine. I'll speak to him this afternoon."

*

The lessons started the following morning. Sara was to meet Daniel in front of the brood-mare barn, but when she arrived, he was nowhere to be seen.

"Do you know where Daniel Riordan is?" she asked a groom.

"He's around the other side of the barn, in the paddock, working with one of the foals," the groom replied, and Sara walked in the designated direction. A trailer was parked inside the fence and one of the grooms was leading a mare up the ramp and into the truck. Daniel followed, leading her foal. The foal's ears flicked back and forth but he went quietly up the ramp after his mother. Daniel closed the trailer gate and Sara walked slowly along the paddock fence. Fergus and Deirdre, who had been lying quietly in the sun, got up and came to her. She murmured to them and they returned to their original positions. Daniel and the groom stood inside the paddock, talking idly, and Sara wondered if she should intrude. As she hesitated at the gate, Daniel glanced over and saw her. He said something to the groom and then walked across the grass to Sara.

"Am I late?" he asked.

"Well, Grandpa said ten o'clock and it's after ten now."

He didn't look at all disturbed. "I'll have someone saddle up right away." He ducked between the white-painted rails and disappeared into the barn. He was back almost immediately. "Lady will be ready in a minute," he said. "Just wait right here until I unload the trailer."

Ducking back into the paddock, Daniel returned to the trailer and opened the tailgate. First the mare and then the foal were led back down the ramp. The two men brought the horses over to the gate where Sara stood.

"Shall I open it for you?" she asked quickly.

"Thank you, Miss Underwood," the groom responded.

Sara swung the gate wide, and the mare and foal walked through. At about the same moment, a groom came out of the barn leading a saddled bay mare on a longe line.

"Jim, you and Frank put the mare and foal back out in the paddock," Daniel said, handing the foal's lead line to the groom who was holding Lady. Daniel took the longe line and said to Sara, "We'll go back into the paddock," and she opened the gate once again.

Daniel put Sara on a big circle, with himself in the middle holding the longe line. Sara felt very high off the ground and extremely awkward, but she found she remembered how to post. The bay mare moved very quietly, obeying all of Daniel's voice commands promptly and smoothly. After thirty minutes he called a halt.

"That's enough for today, I'm thinking. Your muscles will be sore tomorrow."

Sara slid down as she recalled being taught long ago. Her knees buckled slightly as her legs took her weight, and she laughed. "Yes, I see what you mean. But it was fun."

Daniel was running up the stirrups. "You did well."

"Do you really think so?"

Sara was standing on the other side of the horse across from Daniel, and his eyes met hers. She felt her heart jump. His eyes looked very blue against his lean, dark face. She smiled at him a bit tentatively. Her cheeks were lightly flushed with exercise and there was a faint film of perspiration on her forehead and upper lip. "Yes," he said softly, "I do."

"Can we have another lesson tomorrow, then?"

He began to lead the mare toward the barn. "Surely."

Sara trailed after him. "What are you going to do now?"

"Unsaddle Lady, brush her, and turn her out."

"Can I help?"

There was a brief pause and then he answered, "Of course." He spoke, as always, with perfect courtesy. "If you want to."

"What were you doing before, with the mare and the foal?" Sara asked curiously as he put Lady on crossties in the aisle.

"Giving the foal a lesson. He has to learn to load and unload, and it's easier to have him do it with his mother first. He won't forget. Horses have phenomenal memories." He began to unbuckle the girth.

"Show me what you're doing," Sara asked, moving beside him.

She followed Daniel around for the rest of the morning. There was something about him that drew her to him, and it wasn't just his looks. He was so quiet, so calm, so endlessly patient. Sara could clearly understand why he had been put in charge of the foals and the yearlings. She sat on a paddock fence for thirty minutes and watched him teach a young foal to lead away from its mother. When the foal refused to budge, Daniel looped a long lead around his rear; when the line was pulled, the foal's hindquarters were forced forward as well. The foal finally went forward, and Daniel patted him and praised him and gave him a few oats as a reward. It was with extreme reluctance that Sara went back to the house for lunch. She would have liked to spend the rest of the day watching Daniel, but she was afraid of becoming a nuisance.

*

Sara had her lesson the following morning and once again stayed with Daniel until lunch. Then she showered and changed into a lime-green linen dress for her grandfather's lawn party.

The guests were mostly of venerable years, but there were a few younger people in attendance.

William Aronsen made a point of introducing Sara to Mr. and Mrs. Benjamin Debrett and their grandson, B.J. B.J. was a handsome curly-haired young man of about twenty-five, and he appeared to be immediately taken by Sara. He adeptly cut her from the crowd and got her to himself at a table set up under the trees.

"How long have you been here?" he asked. "It can't have been for too long—rumor would have spread." There was a look of unmistakable admiration in his warm brown eyes.

"I've been here only a few days," Sara said in a cool voice. "I came back with Grandpa from New York."

"I hope you're going to stay awhile."

Sara's eyes flickered involuntarily past him toward the barns. "Yes," she murmured, "I believe I am." Her eyes returned to the pleasant, open face of the man opposite her. "I understand your family raises jumpers. Isn't that unusual for this part of Kentucky?"

"It is now, of course. At one time it wasn't, though. My family is one of the few holdouts who haven't gone over to racing on the flat."

"Steeplechasing must be exciting," Sara remarked.

B.J.'s brown eyes shone. "There's nothing else like it. I'd rather ride a steeplechase than anything else in the world. It's the biggest high I know of."

"Isn't it awfully dangerous, though?"

He shrugged. "It's no more dangerous than a lot of other things. And it's a lot more fun."

Sara smiled. "I think my father would have liked you. He used to race cars."

*

Sara spent the greater part of the day with B.J. He was nice and easy to talk to, and he didn't make her uncomfortable by complimenting her too much. The Prince of Bolzano had always showered her with compliments, and she had hated it. It always made her freeze up and assume her haughtiest-looking expression.

Together, Sara and B.J. mingled with the other party guests, and every conversation seemed to revolve around horses.

"Do we sound awfully dull to you?" B.J. asked her. "Horses, horses, and more horses, I mean."

"No," Sara replied, "I think it's interesting. In fact, I think I've caught the fever. I'm even learning how to ride."

"Good for you," he said enthusiastically. "Who's teaching you?"

Sara smiled slightly. "Daniel Riordan."

"Daniel, eh?" B.J. looked at her shrewdly. "He's a good-looking devil, isn't he?"

For some reason, Sara felt wary. She smiled deliberately. "He's too good to be true. The Irish tourist bureau ought to snap him up."

The shrewd look left B.J.'s eyes and he laughed. "He's a great guy, though, under all those fancy looks. He rides for us sometimes, when we have an extra mount. You couldn't have a better teacher."

"Well, it's nice to know I'm in good hands," Sara said lightly. "Did you go to school around here?"

"No," B.J. answered, following her change of subject. "I went to school in Maryland. How about you?"

Sara shrugged. "The usual stuff. I learned how to pour a mean cup of tea."

He grinned, and his eyes sparkled. "Are you doing anything tomorrow night? Would you like to take in dinner and maybe a movie?"

"Sure," Sara said. "It sounds like fun."

The following night, Sara went out with B.J., and they ran into some friends of his at dinner. The next day one of the friends called and asked her out. In a short time, and without the slightest effort on her part, Sara found herself at the center of an ever-widening social circle. The telephone rang persistently, and her grandfather joked about getting Sara her own private line. He was delighted to see her going out with some "decent boys," as he called them, and not a decadent Italian prince. And he said nothing about the amount of time she spent with Daniel.

*

Sara's riding lessons had progressed to the point where Daniel let her off the longe line and gave her reins. He was an exacting and demanding teacher, but his patience was inexhaustible. The only time he ever raised his voice was when she pulled too hard on the reins. "Get off the mare's mouth," he would say sharply, and Sara would hastily loosen her grip.

He was so unhurried. Sara, fresh from the frenetic pace of New York, could not get over how relaxed he was. Nothing seemed to faze him. Nothing made him angry. Or so she thought, until one morning an incident made her realize that he had a temper, after all.

Sara's lesson had finished, and she was leading Lady back to the barn. Daniel was going to show her how to give a horse a bath, and he had gone off to get a bucket and a sponge. As Sara rounded the corner of the barn, one of the grooms was coming along with a wheelbarrow filled with old stall bedding. A stable cat was lying right in the middle of his path, sunning herself. "Hey, you stupid cat," the groom said, "move!" The cat's eyes stayed blissfully closed. Not seeing Sara behind him, the groom yelled something obscene, walked over to the cat, and kicked her hard in the ribs. Sara gave a sharp cry of protest in unison with the cat's screech of pain.

"Fennel." It took Sara a second to recognize Daniel's voice. Looking over to the doorway, she saw him standing there, expressionless. He was very still and his eyes, aimed at the groom, were narrowed. "You can collect your wages now," he said.

The man started to speak and then stopped. Daniel's eyes were like blue ice. Fennel finally turned on his heel and stalked away. "I'll move the wheelbarrow for you," Daniel said stonily, glancing at a stunned Sara.

She watched him in silence as he picked up the wheelbarrow's handles and pushed it over to the manure pile, where he began methodically to shovel out the bedding. He did not look at Sara again. She led Lady into the barn, took off her bridle, and put her on cross ties. Then she gave the mare a carrot and went up to the loft to look for the abused cat.

"Where are you?" It was Daniel's voice coming from below. She had asked him once to call her Sara, but he never had. He had stopped calling her "Miss" however, in deference to her request. They were consequently at the point where he refrained from addressing her by any name at all. It annoyed Sara, and hurt her, but she wasn't going to say anything further. She just pretended she didn't notice.

"I'm up here," she called back. "I'm trying to find Tigey."

There was the sound of feet on the ladder, and first Daniel's head appeared, then his shoulders, followed by the rest of him. "Where is she?" he asked.

"I saw her run up here, but I can't find her. Wait—there she is, over in the corner." Sara pointed up to a rafter.

"Come by me, girl." Daniel's eyes were focused on the cat, and Sara moved softly until she was beside Daniel. He called the cat again, his voice gentle and tender. It was impossible to believe it was the same voice that had been so hard with anger only minutes before. Tigey watched him and didn't move.

It took Daniel fifteen minutes to coax the cat down so he could examine her. He had sent Sara from the loft to tend to Lady, but as she brushed the mare and picked her hooves clean, she listened to Daniel with the cat. When he finally came down the ladder holding Tigey in his arms, Sara felt tears sting her eyes. She blinked, feeling foolish.

"Is she okay?" she asked.

"I think so." His eyes narrowed. "That bloody sod. I'd like to kick him where it hurts."

Sara's eyes widened in surprise. Daniel glanced at her and seemed to realize for the first time who she was. "I'm sorry," he said. "I should have not spoken so."

Sara grinned. "Don't mind me. In fact, I'll double the sentiment."

His face relaxed and he gave her one of his rare smiles. Sara's heart turned completely over. He didn't say anything else, but walked out of the barn with the cat still in his arms. Sara put Lady in her stall, and when she went to look for Daniel, he was gone. She asked a few grooms if they had seen him, but no one had. Dejectedly, she returned to the house. She had an afternoon tennis date, but she would rather have been with Daniel.

Chapter 4

Sara played tennis all afternoon with a young man named David Harley, and that evening she went out to dinner with B. J. Debrett. She managed to bring the conversation around to Daniel without being too obvious.

"I'm actually being allowed to leave the paddock tomorrow," she said lightly to B.J. "Simon Legree has announced that I'm fit to be seen."

B.J. grinned. "You've done it faster than I expected."

"I was ready days ago," she complained. "Daniel just hates the idea of trusting me with one of his precious horses."

"He doesn't want you to get hurt."

"Hah," Sara muttered. "It's not me he's worried about, it's Lady."

At that, B.J. laughed. "That's probably true. Daniel loves his horses. And they're not even his. I can imagine what he'll be like when they really do belong to him."

Sara put her salad fork down. "What do you mean?"

"He's saving money for his own farm in Ireland," B.J. explained as he buttered some garlic bread. "He owns the land already, but he needs money for barns and horses. That's why he came to America—to earn his fortune, you might say. Our ancestors would have approved."

"I didn't know that," Sara said slowly.

"I didn't either until just a few months ago. He's a reticent fellow, Daniel. He's so laid-back and natural that you don't notice it at first, but he's pretty good at keeping his business to himself."

"Evidently," Sara replied. "It's funny, I always thought the Irish were great talkers."

"Oh, Daniel can talk all right—he just doesn't talk about himself." A serious look crossed B.J.'s face. "It isn't easy for a man to look like Daniel, you know."

Sara's eyes glowed golden in the light of the candles. "I should think it would be a distinct advantage."

B.J. shook his head firmly. "No. It's an advantage to be handsome—like me." He leered, and Sara laughed. "But looking like Daniel isn't easy. You attract the wrong sort of men, and the ones like you don't trust you."

"Good heavens," said Sara faintly, "I never thought of that."

"And then, to top it off, nobody will trust their women around you."

"Stop," Sara said. "You're going to make me cry. Poor Daniel."

B.J. sipped his wine. "I wouldn't go as far as that, but I do see how it's made him cautious." He looked at Sara's face in the candlelight. "Are you cautious, Sara honey?"

"Very," Sara replied decisively.

"Damn," B.J. said, and Sara laughed again.

*

Sara had bought a pair of high black field boots in Lexington, and the following morning she wore them in honor of her first real ride. She surveyed herself approvingly in the mirror before going to meet Daniel. The stretch breeches and boots were flattering to her slim figure, she decided. Her long hair was parted in the middle and tied at the nape of her neck. The strong spring sun had tinted her fair skin a pale golden color—the darkest she ever got. She looked neat and tidy and very horsewomanly, she thought. She straightened her belt and headed toward the barn.

Lady was ready but there was no sign of Daniel. "Do you know where he is?" Sara asked the groom who was holding the saddled mare.

"No, miss. He told me to get Lady ready for you, that's all I know. He'll be here soon, I reckon."

The boy's face was expressionless, but Sara caught a hint of something in his voice that made her look at him sharply. He gazed down at his feet, refusing to meet her eyes. Sara stuck her chin in the air. "Bring Lady along to the paddock," she said imperiously, and walked off without looking back.

She rode Lady around the paddock for about twenty minutes before Daniel finally arrived. He was dressed in attire almost identical to hers: boots, breeches, and short-sleeved knit shirt. Daniel's boots were well worn, however, and when he swung into the saddle of the black mare he was to ride, he looked so natural and at home that Sara immediately felt awkward and all wrong.

"Come along, then," he said to her as she walked Lady out through the paddock gate to join him. "We'll go up the road by the mares' paddocks." Sara nodded and the two horses moved off together.

Sara wondered where he had been. "You were late," she said after a while. Then, afraid she had sounded annoyed, she added, "I hope nothing was wrong."

"No," Daniel said comfortably. He turned his head very slightly toward her. "I'm sorry you were kept waiting."

He didn't sound sorry at all, nor was it the first time he had kept her waiting. "I don't think you're a bit sorry," she retorted. "In fact, from watching you operate these past weeks, I don't think you have the slightest concept of time at all."

A look of faint amusement crossed his bronzed face. "Ah well, that's the Catholic point of view for you," he said. "When you have one foot in eternity, the rest of time has little importance."

Sara laughed. "So that's your secret."

"If you want to call it that." He looked directly ahead of him once again, the amusement fading from his face, leaving it grave and remote.

B.J. was right, Sara found herself thinking. One could be perfectly comfortable and natural with Daniel without having any sense of knowing him at all. She wanted to learn more about him, but every time she tried to get past the barrier of his invincible courtesy, she was brought up short. She could count on one hand the number of times she had seen him smile. Sara sighed, and he looked at her.

"Shall we trot?" he asked, and at her assent the two horses moved forward.

On their way home, Sara's mare was stung by a bee. They were walking the horses with loose reins, and Daniel was telling her about the three-year-old her grandfather was sending to New York for the Belmont Stakes, when all of a sudden Lady reared and then bucked. Sara was thrown clear of the animal and landed in the middle of the road, where she lay still for a moment, stunned. As she came to her senses, she realized that Daniel was bending over her. She thought she heard him say her name and she opened her eyes and looked up. His face was very close to hers, and there was concern in his blue eyes.

"I think I'm okay," Sara said shakily.

She started to sit up, and he squatted back on his heels and watched. Sara drew a deep shaken breath, and as she pulled her legs up, Daniel put a restraining hand on her arm. "Sit still for a minute, girl. You're after having the wind knocked out of you."

He was right, but the touch of his hand wasn't helping her regain her breath, either. "What happened?" she asked a little huskily.

"I'm not sure, but I'm thinking maybe something stung the mare."

Sara looked around. Her ribbon had come loose and her long hair was streaming around her shoulders. "Where is she? Is she all right?"

"She's back in the barn now, surely. It's you that's had the worst of it. Can you stand up now?"

"Yes." Sara rose to her feet and staggered a little. He braced her arm with his.

"Are you all right?"

The arm under hers was rock hard. "Yes. Just bruised, I think." Her hair lay fanned against his shoulder, a spangle of brown, red, and gold clinging to the navy jersey material of his shirt.

He didn't step away from her, and she looked up into his face. He was looking at her hair, and then, slowly, his eyes moved to meet hers. Sara's heart dropped into her stomach. At this minute he was as aware of her as she was of him. She could see it in his eyes. She stood perfectly still, afraid to break the spell. Daniel's mare tossed her head impatiently, and Sara saw Daniel take a deep breath before moving away from her.

"You'd better get up on Eastern Star," he said. His voice was calm, but Sara was still close enough to see his pulse beating under the tanned skin of his throat.

"All right," she said, moving toward the horse. She felt oddly shaken, a condition that she could not attribute to her fall.

"I'll give you a leg up," Daniel offered.

Wordlessly she let him throw her into the saddle. He shortened the stirrups for her, and then, going to the mare's head, he took the reins and began to lead them home.

*

"What happened to you?" William Aronsen asked as he met his granddaughter in the front hall of the house.

Sara looked at her dirty breeches. "I fell. Lady got stung by a bee, and off I came."

"Well, you don't seem any the worse for wear."

"No, I didn't get hurt--just a little shook up. Lady is okay, too. She went back to the barn after she dumped me,"

Aronsen grunted. "George Grega called this morning for you."

"Oh?" Sara said indifferently.

Aronsen looked amused. "Don't jump out of your skin."

Sara grinned. "He's a nice-enough guy, Grandpa."

"But B.J. Debrett is nicer?"

"Yes," Sara answered truthfully. "I think he is."

Aronsen smiled with satisfaction and went off to his office. Sara went upstairs to her room and sat on her window seat staring toward the barns. Her grandfather would not be so satisfied if he could see into her mind, she thought ruefully.

She wished Daniel had kissed her. She had always been standoffish with men, but she had wanted Daniel to kiss her. It was the first time she had felt like that, and it was consequently the first time she realized the full extent of his attraction for her. She had sensed it for a long time, but it had only become clear this afternoon when he had gazed at her hair.

She drew her knees up, rested her cheek on them, and looked dreamily off across the acres and acres of rolling grass and white fences. She thought about being in Daniel's arms, of running her fingers through his thick black hair; she thought about kissing him. It was an extremely pleasant dream that kept her occupied until B.J. arrived for their tennis date.

*

Sara had scarcely left the barn before a groom came to find Daniel.

"Rosie's foal is acting funny, Daniel. You'd better come have a look," the worried groom said.

Immediately Daniel drove out to the paddock where Rose of Alba, one of Aronsen's finest brood mares, was turned out with her three-month-old foal.

The baby was indeed in distress, lying on his back and rolling around. He was not even interested in nursing.

"Get Dr. Scott," Daniel ordered. There was a thin line between his brows.

"Red went for him already," the groom replied, and in a few minutes John Scott, the farm's veterinarian, climbed into the paddock.

"Looks like a high impaction," Daniel said.

Dr. Scott examined the foal and then concurred with Daniel's diagnosis. He administered a sedative for the pain and a laxative for the impaction, and the two men waited with the foal until the medication took effect. Once the impacted mass was cleared from the colon, the foal immediately felt better. In a few minutes he was nursing comfortably.

Daniel and John Scott went back to Daniel's cottage for coffee and sandwiches. "I saw you riding with Sara Underwood earlier," the vet said as he sat at the kitchen table and watched Daniel put the kettle on the stove.

"Yes. It was her first time out of the paddock, and wouldn't the luck have it that a bee should sting her horse?"

"Did she take a fall?"

"That she did." Daniel put ham and cheese on some rye bread and brought the sandwiches to the table.

"She wasn't hurt, was she?" Dr. Scott asked with interest.

"No, just a wee bit shook up."

"That's good. Bill Aronsen wouldn't be pleased to have his granddaughter smashed up. I think he's settling his dynastic hopes on Sara. It's pretty obvious by now that her mother isn't going to give him a grandson."

Daniel poured the hot water into cups and stirred in instant coffee. He placed the cups on the table and sat opposite the vet. "I suppose not," he remarked unconcernedly.

"She's a stunning-looking girl, but she sure has her nose in the air." John Scott's kind, weathered countenance faced Daniel. "Except with you," he added.

Daniel looked up quickly and met the vet's worried gray eyes. John Scott had been one of the first friends Daniel had made at Canfield Farm. "She's always looking for you," he said to Daniel. "The boys think it's rather funny."

Daniel frowned. "Are people talking?"

"Yes. You've always been so careful, Daniel. Too careful, I've always thought. But now is not the time to relax your guard."

Daniel's mouth set. "Well, what am I to do?" he asked impatiently. "She's the boss's granddaughter, John. I can't simply tell her to get lost."

"It's precisely because she is the boss's granddaughter that you'd better tell her," Dr. Scott said bluntly. "I'd hate to see you out of a job over this, Daniel. But it could happen, if Aronsen thought you were screwing around with his granddaughter."

An angry flush darkened Daniel's face. "I'm not screwing around with her," he said tightly.

"I know you're not." The vet's voice was reassuring. "But let's face it, Daniel, you're twenty-six years old, you know what you look like, and the girl is chasing you so hard that all the grooms are talking. If word gets to Aronsen, what do you suppose he's going to think?"

Daniel stared at the tabletop in silence. After a long moment, he picked up his coffee with a steady hand and sipped it. "She isn't chasing me," he said.

"Daniel, everywhere you are, there she is, too. When she's not junketing off with B.J. Debrett, that is."

Daniel put his cup down. "You know, John," he said slowly, "I'm not so sure that she isn't just a little innocent after all?"

The vet snorted eloquently. "Come on, Daniel. With that mother and that upbringing? You must be kidding. She was hanging around with some Italian prince before Aronsen dragged her away from New York."

"So I've heard," Daniel said expressionlessly.

"Listen to me, boy." Scott leaned toward Daniel. "I'm not one to butt in on other folk's business, you know that. But will you think about what I've said?"

Daniel's eyes met his fully, but their expression was veiled. "I'll do that," he promised, and with mutual relief the two men changed the subject of conversation.

Chapter 5

When Sara went down to the barn the following morning for her ride, Daniel wasn't there. "Daniel's working with the yearlings this morning, Miss Underwood," the red-haired groom told her. "He asked me to ride along with you today."

Sara made an effort to hide her disappointment. "All right," she said graciously. "Thank you." "No problem. If you want to take Lady into the paddock, I'll be with you in a minute." "Fine."

Sara's second ride was smooth and uneventful. She enjoyed being out on a horse, but she missed Daniel. They rode around practically the whole farm, but she didn't see Daniel anywhere.

After they returned, Sara lingered around the barn to give Lady a bath. She had almost finished when the sound of footsteps made her look around hopefully. But it was only Dr. Scott.

"Good morning, Miss Underwood," the vet said, strolling toward her. "Did you have a nice ride?"

"Yes, thank you." Sara finished Lady's last hoof and straightened up. She had met Dr. Scott a few times, and he had always given her the feeling that he didn't approve of her. "It was more successful than yesterday's, at any rate. At least I didn't fall off."

The vet smiled slightly. He was a big, burly man in his early forties. "You ought to get B.J. to ride with you," he suggested. "He might even teach you to jump."

"I don't think I'm as advanced as all that," Sara said.

"You never know." The vet gave her a hard, level look. "Well, have a good day, Miss Underwood."

By now it was perfectly plain to Sara that Dr. Scott did not like her. She raised her chin. "Thank you, Doctor." The cool look in her eyes and the curve of her mouth made her look faintly insolent. "You too."

The vet nodded curtly and walked into the barn. Sara untied Lady from the fence and took her to the paddock where she was usually turned out.

Then she sat with her back against the white planks, watching the horses graze. She had almost dozed off when a dog's nose poked into her back, waking her abruptly. It was Deirdre. Sara turned around and saw Daniel walking down the road. She got to her feet, and seeing her, he stopped abruptly. Then he continued on slowly.

"Deirdre, girl come here," he called. He nodded to Sara. "Good morning. And how was your ride?"

"Very nice." She moved to join him on the road. "I stayed on the whole time."

"Good." He continued to walk, and Sara fell into step beside him. She sensed something different about him, and she looked sideways at him from under her lashes. A lock of black hair had fallen forward over his forehead and there was a streak of dirt on one high cheekbone.

"You look like you were working hard," she said.

"Yes."

"Are you breaking the yearlings? Can I watch?"

"Well, now," he said easily, "if I were you, I'd go watch the two-year-olds being worked. Dave Bean is in charge of them while Henry is in New York. This is a racing farm as well as a breeding farm, and you've seen only one half of the operation. Surely your grandfather would like you to see it all."

Sara bent her head and looked at the toes of her boots. He glanced over at her quickly. The nape of her neck under her hair was still white as milk, in contrast to the pale golden hue of the rest of her skin. Daniel's mouth tightened, and he looked at his dogs.

"Yes," Sara said in a low voice. "I guess you're right."

*

Sara's grandfather was pleased as punch with her. She had been a quiet, sullen child and it delighted him to see that she had turned out so well. His doctor had recently issued strict orders about his patient's high blood pressure, and for the first time, Sara's grandfather was giving serious thought to the future. Lorraine had been a severe disappointment to him, but it was beginning to look as if he might have struck gold in Sara.

He was delighted that she got on so well with B.J. Debrett. In fact, Aronsen spent almost as much time daydreaming about B.J. and his granddaughter as Sara spent daydreaming about herself and someone quite different.

Both B.J. and Daniel were quite busy during the next few days, and Sara scarcely saw either of them. Daniel was working on the farm, and B.J. was helping his family prepare for the Lexington Hunt Cup race meeting, which was to be run on the Debrett estate, Inverlochy, the following week.

"It's a rather well-known occasion," B.J. explained to Sara one evening when he found the time to take her out to dinner. "There are six races in all, but the big event of the day is the Lexington Hunt Cup. It's a recognized race, which means it's run under the rules of the National Steeplechase and Hunt Association. There's a pretty decent cash prize too, although it can't compare with the money offered at flat races, of course."

"Grandpa says there's no money in steeplechasing."

"There isn't," BJ. replied cheerfully. They were eating steak at his favorite restaurant. "Diehard steeplechase people aren't in it for the money. You have to have money to go in for it, though—that I will admit." He took a bite of his rare sirloin. "There was a time when a lot of the big Kentucky farms raised jumpers, but during the sixties nearly all of them moved over onto the flat. Steeplechasing became a bit of an eccentricity in the States. It's still big in England, though." He grinned at Sara. "The dream of my life is to ride one day in the Grand National."

Sara returned his smile. "Perhaps you will."

"You're coming over for the race next week, aren't you?"

"Of course. Who are you riding?"

"Lara. She's the mare I won the Maryland Hunt Cup on last year. This year we came in second."

Sara sipped her wine and nodded in commiseration.

"Daniel's going to ride Coverdale in the Hunt Cup. He's the big bay gelding Miles Foreman passed on to me a few months ago. Miles had trouble showing him as a hunter, but I think he's going to find his niche in steeple chasing. At any rate, if the horse has it in him, Daniel will find it."

Sara's hand stilled. "I'll have two of you to root for, then."

B.J. put his hand over hers. "You root for me, honey. You root for me."

*

The day of the celebrated event was cool and overcast, but the weather did not seem to affect the spirits of the local residents, who turned out in droves to watch. There were tailgate parties all over the lawns of Inverlochy. B.J. showed Sara the course, which was three miles long and made up of timber and brush fences averaging about five feet in height. It looked extremely dangerous to her.

"Not at all," B.J. said when she expressed these sentiments to him. He glanced over her head and suddenly waved. "Daniel! Over here."

Sara turned her head and when she saw Daniel coming toward them, her heart began to race.

"Quite a turnout, B.J.," Daniel remarked amiably as he reached them. He nodded to Sara. Both he and B.J. wore light-colored breeches, riding boots, and identically striped jackets, which Sara assumed were in the Debrett colors.

"Grandpa's pleased. We're just going for some coffee. Come with us," B.J. said to Daniel.

Daniel obligingly fell into step with them, and the three went along to the table where Mrs. Debrett, B.J.'s grandmother, was dispensing lunch.

"Sit down," she invited. "How about a lobster-salad sandwich, Sara? I know the boys aren't eating until after the race."

Sara accepted the sandwich and looked curiously at the young men sitting next to her. Neither of them was particularly big, but on the other hand, they certainly weren't small either. "I would have thought both of you would be too heavy to ride in a race," she said.

"Jump jockeys can weigh considerably more than flat jockeys," B.J. explained. "The usual weight allowance for amateurs is one hundred and sixty-five pounds, and Daniel and I can do that without much problem."

Sara looked sideways at Daniel, slim and brown beside her on the picnic bench. "Do women ever compete?" she asked.

"Surely," Daniel answered. "In fact, there's a ladies' race on the card for today."

"Oh. Then the women don't compete directly with the men?"

Daniel looked slightly amused. "Is it *National Velvet* you're thinking of?"

Sara smiled. "I suppose so. And I know there are women jockeys on the flat."

"Women can ride in steeplechases," B.J. said. "Not too many do, though. You have to be extremely fit, and you can't be afraid of falling."

Sara thought of the fences B.J. had shown her. "How can you not be afraid of falling?" she asked faintly.

"When you worry about falling, it's time to stop racing," B.J. said cheerfully. Daniel's black head nodded in agreement.

*

The Lexington Hunt Cup race was like nothing Sara had ever seen. The spectators stood on a hilly rise of grass outside the timber rail fence that enclosed the course. There were twelve horses in the field, and by the time they were halfway around the course, six of them were down. Sara couldn't believe how dangerous it looked, and stared in horror as Daniel's horse stretched out in midair to clear a man on the ground. Both Daniel and B.J. were still in the saddle, however, as they approached the last two fences. B.J. cleared the final fence first and settled down to ride hard for the finish. Daniel's horse jumped cleanly and stretched out to try and catch the leading mare.

The people all around Sara were cheering and she could hear her grandfather call, surprisingly, "Come on, Daniel! Move him!" Coverdale was slowly gaining ground on the mare. Come on, Daniel, come on! Sara rooted him on silently but intensely. But there wasn't enough time, and as they crossed the finish line, B.J.'s horse was still a neck ahead.

There was champagne back at the picnic table. "That was a damn fine ride," B.J. told Daniel.

"It surely was," Mr. Debrett said. "That horse has been a holy terror for Miles Forman."

"He's a very strong jumper," Daniel replied.

"He needs to learn a few things, but I think he's your next Maryland Cup horse, B.J."

"I can't believe you can actually get a horse to do that," Sara said. "You'd think they'd refuse to jump, particularly after they've fallen once or twice."

"A good steeplechaser loves it as much as we do," Daniel explained.

"You bet." B.J. glanced at his grandfather. "Remember Firebet, Grandpa?"

"I sure do. I'll never forget that race for as long as I live."

"What happened?" Sara asked.

"It was the 1949 Belmont Grand National," Mr. Debrett said. "Firebet lost his rider at the first fence, but it never crossed that horse's mind to quit. He went right on racing, jumped all his fences, and paced himself perfectly. He was at the end of the field as they came into the backstretch, and then he decided it was time to make his move. As they rounded the final turn, he was in third place, and as they jumped the last fence, he was neck and neck with the-leader. He crossed the finish line first."

"How marvelous," Sara said, thrilled.

"Yep. I've always thought it was a shame that the rules wouldn't allow him to claim the win. He deserved it."

B.J. raised his champagne glass. "To Firebet," he said, and everyone laughed and drank.

It was a festive and happy party and it seemed everyone Sara had ever met in Kentucky was there.

Sara noticed how perfectly at ease Daniel appeared in that jovial group of millionaires. Nor did anyone attempt to condescend to him. He was part of the magical community of the horse and consequently he belonged.

He was standing next to B.J.'s grandmother when Sara went up to him.

"Are you enjoying yourself, Sara?" Mrs. Debrett asked.

"Very much. It's been a little disheartening, though. I thought I was riding very well, and then seeing these riders today ... well, it's put me in my place."

"B.J. tells me you've been taking lessons." Mrs. Debrett smiled at Daniel, and Sara couldn't help thinking that even old women took on a certain glow when they were around him. "How's she doing, Daniel?" B.J.'s grandmother asked.

"Very nicely, indeed. She has good balance and nice light hands."

Sara felt absurdly pleased. "He shouts at me if I hang on Lady's mouth," she told Mrs. Debrett. "I'd better have light hands."

"Don't be telling tales to Mrs. Debrett," Daniel said reproachfully. "I never shouted at you."

"Get off the mare's mouth!" Sara said in a good imitation of his accent.

He looked at her for a moment and then his face broke into its rare smile. "Sure and it's a good thing you've never heard me when I really shout."

"You never really shout, Daniel," Mrs. Debrett said. "I always thought the Irish were a roaring, rowdy race until I met you."

"Ah, the Irish are a race of saints and poets, Mrs. Debrett," he replied charmingly, "with the odd horseman thrown in here and there."

"No need to ask which you are, Daniel," the old woman said with a smile.

He shook his head. "No. No need at all."

B.J. insisted on taking Sara home, but when he tried to kiss her in the car, she eluded him and got out.

"Sara..." he said plaintively.

She slammed the car door and went around to the driver's window. "Thank you for a lovely day," she said to him. "I enjoyed it very much."

"I won the Hunt Cup," he said. "You could at least give me a kiss for that."

"To the victor belongs the spoils?" she inquired mockingly. "Oh no, Mr. Debrett. You got your cup. That's quite enough for one day, I think."

"Sara..." He reached out the window and grabbed her arm.

She smiled into his frustrated brown eyes. "Well, just one," she said softly, and leaning down, she kissed him lightly on the mouth. She stepped back from the car door and he released her. "Good night, B.J.," she said, and walked sedately up the stairs and into the house.

The problem was that it wasn't B.J. she wanted to kiss, Sara thought as she readied herself for bed. She liked B.J. very much, but he wasn't the man she wanted to kiss.

Sara arose very early the following morning and went downstairs to have a cup of coffee with her grandfather. They were both going to the training track to watch the two-year-olds have their early-morning workouts.

"I have great hopes for Bold Decision," Aronsen told her as they drove together to the track. "I think he'll cop all the two-year-old races this fall. Never seen a horse run like him—effortless, like the wind."

The early-morning air was damp and chilly, and Sara shoved her hands into the pockets of her sweatjacket as she and her grandfather stood along the rail and watched the two-year-olds race down the track.

Dave Bean joined them. "Spendthrift was down with colic last night," he said to Aronsen.

Sara's grandfather frowned. "Bad?" he asked sharply.

"He's going to be all right, I think. John and Daniel were with him all night."

"I'll go by and see him," Aronsen said decisively. "Come along, Sara."

They got into the car and drove toward the yearling barns. "What's colic?" Sara asked.

"It's a digestive ailment. It's also the number-one horse killer in the country."

Sara looked over at her grandfather's craggy profile. "What causes it?"

He grunted. "A lot of things." He pulled the car up by the barn and got out, leaving Sara to follow.

Daniel was walking Spendthrift around the back paddock. He still wore yesterday's boots and breeches, and Sara realized with a start that he hadn't even been home to change. He walked over to them, the horse moving slowly behind him on a lead line.

"How is he?" Aronsen asked gruffly.

"He's all right now, sir. I was just going to put him in his stall. He's tired."

"What caused the colic?"

"Cribbing. We're going to have to wire up his stall, I'm afraid."

Aronsen nodded. "Spendthrift isn't the only one who looks tired."

Daniel smiled very faintly. "It was a long night."

"Sara will drive you home," her grandfather said. He put out an imperative hand and took the lead line. "Take the day off, boy, and go to bed."

"Thank you, sir. I'll do that."

"Here you are, Sara," Aronsen said, handing her the car keys. "You can come back for me after you've dropped Daniel off."

"Okay, Grandpa." She looked at Daniel. "The car's out front."

Silently he got into the car beside her. Sara backed out of the drive and turned the car onto the main farm road. She knew which cottage Daniel lived in; he had pointed it out to her on their first and only ride.

It was a three-minute ride, and after Sara parked the car in front of the small white-painted house, she turned in her seat to look at the man next to her. He was unshaven, and his face looked drawn with fatigue.

"Were you really walking that horse all night?" she asked softly.

"Yes." He rubbed his stubble. "You can't let a colicking horse lie down."

"Poor Daniel." Impulsively she reached over and placed her hand over his where it lay on the seat between them. "You look so tired," she said.

She felt his hand grow rigid beneath hers. His heavy lids lifted, and he looked directly into her face. Her lovely full mouth looked very soft. She was bent toward him, and he knew that if he kissed her now, she would respond. She might even come into the cottage with him...but he recalled John Scott's words, took a deep breath, and pulled his hand away. Then, because she attracted him so strongly, and because he was so tired, he was much crueler to her than he had ever meant to be.

"Be a good girl," he said to Sara, "and leave me alone."

Sara froze. The image of a wild animal who has just spotted a predator flashed into his mind. His black brows came together in a sharp frown, and the look in his eyes changed. Then Sara pulled away from him and stared out the front windshield. "Whatever made you think I was interested?" she asked coolly. "You can get out now."

He hesitated for just a minute, then opened the car door.

"Thanks for the ride," he said.

Sara did not reply, and as soon as the car door closed, she took off in a spray of dirt.

Chapter 6

"Be a good girl and leave me alone." The words ran around and around in Sara's mind all day. She was a nuisance to him. He thought she was chasing him. Perhaps it had seemed that way, but she hadn't meant... Sara's cheeks grew hot with humiliation as she looked back over the past few weeks and realized how her behavior must have appeared to Daniel. How tired he must have become of her trailing him around.

Well, she would do as he had asked and leave him strictly alone. She would go out with B.J.—who seemed to want her company—and with her other friends. She would forget that Daniel Riordan existed.

Sara managed to keep herself busy through the next several weeks. She spent her mornings on the telephone and her afternoons lunching or swimming, playing tennis or riding with B.J. over at Inverlochy. She was careful not to go near the barns or the horses at Canfield. She was too afraid of meeting Daniel. She knew she could not bear to be close to him, that it would hurt too much... *Be a good girl and leave me alone.*

*

There was a crowd of young people around the Harleys' pool one hot afternoon when Linda Freeland said, "Why don't we all go dancing over at the Digs tonight?"

Her suggestion met with general enthusiasm and Sara said "Sure" when B.J. asked if she wanted to go. It really didn't matter much where she went or what she did these days. All the interest seemed to have gone out of her life.

She dressed for the evening in a mauve-colored sundress and for a change let her hair fall loosely about her shoulders. B.J. picked her up at eight-thirty and she smiled at his compliment and got into the front seat of his blue sports car.

"We're picking up Daniel," B.J. said cheerfully, and Sara's heart skipped a beat.

"Oh?" she managed to get out. "How did that happen?"

"Linda invited him along." He grinned in the fading light. "Linda's been inviting Daniel along for two years now. Most of the time he doesn't come—but tonight he said he would."

Sara clenched her hands tightly in her lap. "Then why doesn't Linda pick him up?"

"We're taking Linda too," B.J. said, pulling up in front of Daniel's cottage. He honked the horn and in less than a minute Daniel came out the front door and was walking toward them over the grass. He got into the backseat of the car.

"Glad you decided to come along for a change," B.J. said over his shoulder. "All this 'you are the master, I am the servant,' crap you indulge in is a pain in the ass."

"Ah, you're a fine specimen of a democrat, B.J. Debrett." Daniel's voice, unheard for over two weeks, caused little shivers to go up and down Sara's back.

"Don't ever let my grandpa hear you say that," B.J. retorted. "We're Republicans, my fine Irish friend."

"Same thing," Daniel returned imperturbably, and B.J. laughed.

Linda lived in a big white Colonial house on the outskirts of Lexington. Her family was not in the horse business; her father was a lawyer. She too wore a sundress, and as she got into the car next to Daniel she assumed a distinctly proprietary air. Once or twice as they drove into Lexington, Sara caught the ghost of a grin on B.J.'s mouth. He evidently found the whole scene in the backseat very funny. Sara did not.

The Digs was a disco-style bar with a loud band and a lot of smoke. Sara ordered a Tom Collins and nursed it for half of the evening. She danced with B.J. and with a few of the other young men in their party. There was a lot of noise and laughter and everyone seemed to be in high spirits. Everyone except Sara, who was miserable.

She never looked at Daniel. She didn't have to look at Daniel; she knew his looks by heart: that slim, hard-muscled young man with the face of an archangel. Linda was trying hard to assert ownership, but a few other girls were giving her competition. Sara sipped the water left in the bottom of her drink and tried to listen to what B.J. was saying. The band began to play a slow Lionel Richie song and Sara felt a hand on her arm.

"Dance with me?" said Daniel's voice close to her ear.

Startled, Sara glanced up at him. His face was very close to hers. Sara felt her heart begin to race.

She hesitated; but there was no way she could refuse him with B.J. and the others looking on. "Sure," she said, and standing up hastily, preceded him out to the dance floor. He took her in his arms and drew her close to him. Sara's body was stiff and unyielding under his hands. They danced in silence, Sara terribly conscious of the feel of his body against hers, the hardness of his shoulder under her hand. She wanted the dance to be over with, and at the same time she longed for it to go on forever.

The last beats of the music died away and Daniel said, "Come outside with me for a minute."

"No," Sara said, and looked back toward their table. But Daniel kept her hand in his and began to walk toward the doorway. After a split second's indecision, Sara went with him.

It was warm outside, away from the air conditioning, and the scent of newly cut grass was in the air. They stopped on the edge of the parking lot under a light and Sara looked at the man who had brought her here. She was wearing high-heeled sandals and her eyes were almost on a level with his.

"What do you want?" she asked stiffly. In the light of the overhead lamp her golden eyes looked guarded.

"I want to apologize to you," Daniel said gravely. "I did you an injustice and I'm sorry for it."

A gleam of some indefinable emotion flared in her eyes before the familiar safety curtain of indifference came down.

"That's okay," she said. She looked off across the parking lot, presenting him with an admirable view of her profile. "It's nice to get a breath of fresh air for a minute," she added.

"Yes. I hate places like this. I only came this evening to see you."

She turned her head toward him in surprise.

"Sara..." he said. No one had ever said her name like that before. It sounded like a love word. "I've missed you, girl."

"I was only following your request to stay away." She wasn't looking at him now.

"I know. It's a stupid man I am, Sara Underwood. I made a mistake. Will you forgive me and come help me break the yearlings to saddle tomorrow?" Then, as she stared at him, uncertain, "I won't turn on you again. I promise."

Sara felt tears sting behind her eyes. "I didn't mean to get in your way," she said.

"I know." He smoothed the silky drift of hair from her forehead and then held her face between his thin brown hands. "I was right all along. You're nothing but a little girl after all."

Sara was not feeling the least bit like a little girl at the moment. "I'll be twenty-four in two months," she said.

He grinned, a rare, boyish smile. "Well, now, aren't you getting to be quite the old lady?"

Suddenly Sara felt very happy. She wrinkled her nose at him. "You're not exactly an old coot yourself."

"I'm at least a thousand years older than you," he told her. "Come along, or B.J. will be sending out a search party."

"Linda will be leading it," she said, and shot him a charmingly mischievous look.

His eyes narrowed a little as he looked at her face. "And the next time I ask you to dance, don't stiffen up like a poker."

They had reached the door of the disco. "Ask me again and find out," Sara said smartly, and they both went back into the din of the discotheque.

He did ask her again toward the end of the evening, and this dance was indeed different from their first. He held her lightly but closely, and Sara's body, relaxed and supple, easily followed his every movement. Her eyes grew heavy and languid. Some of the couples were dancing with their arms locked about each other—the girls' around the boys' necks, the boys' around the girls' waists. Sara thought she would like to dance like that with Daniel. She would like to go on dancing with Daniel forever....

The music died away and slowly Daniel dropped his arms. They looked at each other for a moment in silence; then he said, "Come along back to the table."

Sara nodded dreamily and let him guide her back to their noisy group of friends.

The whole color of the evening had changed for Sara. Earlier she had been afraid to look at Daniel; now she made excuses so she could look at him. The rest of the party became merely a backdrop against which this one man was silhouetted. She listened for the sound of his voice even as she nodded in agreement to something B.J. was saying to her. She watched the movement of Daniel's thin muscular hand on the table intently. When B.J. asked her a question she tilted her head toward him a little, pushed a shimmering strand of hair off her forehead with a slow, languid hand, and murmured dreamily, "I beg your pardon, B.J. I didn't hear you."

There was a strangely taut look on B.J.'s handsome face as he looked back at her. He didn't answer, but reached out and put a caressing hand on the smooth skin of her bare shoulder. "Sara..." he said huskily.

Sara recognized the look in his eyes, and it provoked her usual response. She drew back from him a little and said coolly, "Yes?"

B.J. stared in silence at her suddenly remote and slightly haughty face. That look of Sara's had fooled men more worldly than B.J. Sara's reputation in New York was that of a spoiled, sophisticated, slightly bored young debutante. B.J., who was less worldly but more sensitive than Sara's New York crowd, was beginning to sense the fear and insecurity concealed behind that face of hers.

"I won't eat you," he said after a minute.

Sara started to make a flip reply and then stopped. B.J. was very serious. "You looked as if you wanted to," she replied honestly.

He smiled a little, although his eyes remained grave. "Maybe I did, but I would never do anything to hurt or frighten you, Sara. Believe me when I say that."

Sara made a little face. "You're the second person tonight to see what an insecure mess I am. I must be slipping."

The band, which had been on a break, chose this moment to come roaring back. "The second person?" B.J. shouted to her over the din.

"What?" Sara shrieked back.

It was hopeless. "Forget it," B.J. mouthed at her, and she smiled at him ruefully, secretly grateful for the interruption. The conversation had become too personal for her comfort.

They dropped Linda off at her house first. Daniel saw her to the door, then came back and got into the backseat of B.J.'s car.

"There are times, Daniel, when not owning a car can be a distinct advantage," B.J. said wickedly.

"Ah, she's not a bad girl after all," Daniel's voice said out of the darkness. "Just a trifle…smothering."

B.J. chuckled. "Linda wouldn't be a bad deal for you, you know. Her daddy has the biggest law practice in Lexington."

"Good for him," Daniel retorted amiably. "Can you picture Linda on a farm in Ireland, B.J.?"

"If you were there, she'd love it."

"Go on with you. She's a nice girl, but not for the likes of me."

"Well, what girl *is* for the likes of you?" B.J. asked unexpectedly. "You could date dozens of girls in Lexington if you wanted to—you must know that."

"I'm saving my money," Daniel replied peacefully. "We weren't all born stinking rich, my boy."

"That's true enough," B.J. returned. "Touche—once again." He glanced over at Sara, who had been silent throughout this exchange. "Never get into an argument with an Irishman, Sara. He'll have the last word every time."

Sara smiled faintly, but didn't reply. She didn't turn her head either, but she knew Daniel's eyes were on her profile. She could feel him looking at her. Her lashes came down very slowly until they half-screened her eyes. The faint smile remained in the corners of her wide, full mouth. B.J. continued to talk and she let his words roll over her, occasionally murmuring a reply when it seemed necessary.

They let Daniel off at his cottage next. He stood for a minute next to Sara's window and spoke his thanks to B.J.

"Anytime," B.J. said cheerfully. "Chauffeur and baby-sitter par excellence, that's me."

"I'll remember that, boy. Good night, Sara." For a brief moment his eyes met hers; then he was gone into the darkness.

"What did you mean—baby-sitter?" Sara asked B.J. as they drove down the farm road toward her grandfather's house.

"Daniel called and asked me to drive him and Linda. Linda has a car and she was going to pick him up, but our Daniel didn't want to be alone with her. He doesn't really like Linda, although he's far too polite to come right out and say so." B.J. pulled up in front of the house and turned to Sara. "I don't know why he even bothered to come tonight."

"Perhaps he was getting a little lonely."

"No." B.J. sounded very sure of himself. "Daniel is the least lonely person I have ever known. I love horses and farm life just as much, but I'd go crazy leading the confined life he does. He's completely self-sufficient, Daniel is. That's what makes him such an extraordinary guy."

"He doesn't usually go out with women?" Sara couldn't resist the question.

"Not much. There was some gossip a while back about Daniel and an older woman, but he stays pretty clear of girls his own age."

"What woman?" Sara asked immediately.

B.J. grinned. "I'm not about to say, honey. I have very good reason to think the gossip was true, though." He leaned a little toward her. "Why all this interest in Daniel?"

"It's impossible not to be interested in Daniel," Sara answered truthfully.

"Well, try being interested in me for now," he said, and drew her toward him.

Sara let him kiss and hold her, but after a minute she withdrew. "It's late," she said softly.

"God, Sara," B.J. almost groaned, "what does a guy have to do get to first base with you?"

Sara drew a deep breath. "I like you, B.J. Really I do. It's just..." Her voice trailed away and she looked at him worriedly.

"All right, honey." He put his hands on either side of her face and kissed her mouth lightly. "It's all right." He frowned a little. "How did you fend off the Italian prince?"

Sara grinned. "He called me the Snow Queen. I was a challenge to him, I think."

B.J. got out of the car and came around to open her door. "Well, all right, Snow Queen," he said. "You're safely home to Grandpa."

He was so nice, Sara thought gratefully as she went up the stairs to her bedroom. So nice and so kind. She wasn't used to men who were as thoughtful as B.J. If it weren't for Daniel, she might very well let herself fall in love.

Daniel. Never had she felt for anyone what she felt for Daniel. Just dancing with him had turned all her bones to water. She had always been so cautious with men, so afraid she would go down her mother's road. She had sometimes wondered if perhaps she were frigid.

But she wouldn't be frigid with Daniel. She knew that with utter certitude. Daniel. She got into bed and fell asleep to dream of him.

*

Sara rose early the following morning, dressed in jeans and a T-shirt, had some fruit for breakfast, and went out into the warm sunshine. She decided to walk the mile or so from the house to the yearling barn. It would be nice to have a dog to keep her company, she thought as she strode easily along the road. Of course, her mother would never let a dog near her eighteenth-century antiques, but perhaps if she stayed here in Kentucky with her grandfather, she could get one. She would ask him tonight, she decided.

There was a slight sheen of sweat on her forehead and nose when she reached the yearling barn. The inside of the barn was cool and dark in contrast to the hot sunshine outside. There was no sign of Daniel, and Sara went around the stalls, speaking to each of the youngsters. They were alert and curious, and having finished their breakfast, were looking to be turned out to play.

Sara heard footsteps and turned to see Daniel coming down the wide center aisle of the barn. "Good morning," he said. "Have they all finished their feed?"

"Yes. There isn't a trace of hay or grain left anywhere," Sara reported. She looked at him expectantly. "What are you going to do?"

"Today they're going to get their first feel of a saddle."

"Oh my." Sara's eyes widened. "Will they buck and try to throw you?"

His eyes narrowed with amusement. "This isn't the rodeo, girl. And these are thoroughbreds, not wild range horses. We bring them along very slowly. I won't get into the saddle for at least another week."

"Oh." Sara didn't mind at all that he found her ignorance funny. "But I know you've been working with them already. What have you been doing if you haven't been riding them?"

"Driving them on foot in long reins. We do that to teach them to respond to rein signals and to keep their bodies straight. They've also learned to wear a simple bit."

"Do you do all the training yourself, Daniel?" There were at least twenty-four yearlings in the barn.

"Yes. Red helps me—you need someone at the horses' heads—but basically I do it all." He gave her a grave yet kindly look. "Today you're going to help me."

"I am?" Unconsciously Sara stood up straighter. "What do you want me to do?"

"I want you to stand at their heads and distract them with handfuls of oats while I put the saddles on."

Sara could feel her heart pumping harder. "Okay." She tried to sound casual. "When do we start?"

"Right now." He went to the front of the barn and lifted a lightweight saddle. Then he went over to the first stall. "Come along," he said. "We do it in the stall."

"Oh." Sara hurried up the aisle.

"Get a handful of grain from the bin."

"Okay." Sara did as she was instructed and returned to find Daniel talking softly to Executive Suite, the occupant of the first stall. He let the colt sniff the saddle.

"Come in," he said to Sara, "and take hold of his halter." Sara did as she was told, and Daniel moved back alongside the colt. "Show him the grain now."

As the colt thrust his muzzle into Sara's hand, Daniel lowered the saddle onto his back. Executive Suite's ears pricked forward, then back, and his head went up.

"It's all right, fella," Sara murmured. "It's all right. Look. Don't you want some of this nice grain?" She rattled the feed invitingly in her hand and after a minute the colt lowered his head and began to eat. When he had finished, Sara stroked his nose and talked to him. After about two minutes Daniel removed the saddle and came forward to praise and play with the colt. Then he opened the stall door and he and Sara stepped back into the aisle.

"Was that it?" Sara asked in amazement.

"That's it for Executive Suite—for today at least. Now we do the same thing to every other horse in the barn. Tomorrow we leave the saddle on for a little longer, the next day longer still, until finally we add the irons and attach the girth. Then we drive him in long lines with the saddle on him. And only then do I get into the saddle."

"I had no idea it was such a long process," Sara said.

"It's not that long, actually. At the end of a month they should be walking, trotting, and cantering under saddle. Now, get another handful of grain and we'll put a saddle on Fair Play."

"All right." And Sara hurried to do his bidding.

Chapter 7

Sara helped Daniel with the yearlings all through the following week. "Daniel's extraordinary, Grandpa," she said over dinner one evening. "He seems to have a sixth sense about just how much a horse can tolerate before he becomes bored or aggravated. He works each one for a different amount of time."

"Daniel is top-notch when it comes to handling youngsters," Aronsen replied. "Henry trusts him completely—never interferes with the way he breaks the horses. He's broken all our yearlings for the past three years." Aronsen looked up from under his heavy eyebrows at his granddaughter. "He's a damned good-looking fellow, Daniel."

"Mmm," Sara replied carelessly. "He certainly is."

"You seem to be spending an awful lot of time with him."

"I enjoy watching him work the horses," Sara replied. Then, to distract her grandfather from what was becoming an uncomfortable conversation, "I got a letter from Mother today."

"Humph. I see she finally got rid of the golfer."

"Yes. She said she might come out to Kentucky for a visit next month."

"She wants to make sure I'm not getting too fond of you," Aronsen said cynically.

Sara knew this was true. She looked at her grandfather seriously and said, "You wouldn't do anything so Victorian as cutting Mother out of your will, would you, Grandpa?"

There was a grim look about his mouth. "I don't know, Sara. Lorraine has been a grave disappointment to me. I'm beginning to wonder if she's to be trusted with the control of a fortune."

"You could set up trusts or something," Sara suggested.

He looked at her closely. "Or I could leave it to you."

Sara shook her head vigorously. "Oh no. Mother would never forgive me if you did that."

"Do you really care, Sara? It doesn't seem as though Lori has been much of a mother to you. She was too busy gadding about the world to have time for a child. She only had you as a way of keeping Johnny from racing."

Sara's face took on its careful, shuttered look. "I didn't know that."

Aronsen drank some water. "Maybe I shouldn't have said that, but you're a big girl now. I didn't want Lorraine to marry Johnny Underwood, but nothing I could say would stop her. Then, as soon as she had him, she set about trying to change him. He was a racing-car driver. All right, I didn't like that, but that's what he was, and Lori knew it when she married him. He didn't pretend he was going to change professions. But she couldn't take it. First she tried to persuade him to stop, then she had you to tie him down, and finally she ended up divorcing him."

Sara's face had subtly altered as her grandfather spoke. Now she said very softly, "Did she love him?"

"I sometimes think he was the only person Lori has ever loved. But she was selfish even in love." The old man made a rueful face. "She takes after me, I guess. I shouldn't be so hard on her." His hands crashed down on the table, causing the silver and china to jump. "If only she weren't so damned stupid!"

"Didn't you like my father?" Sara asked in an expressionless voice.

"I liked him very much."

Sara looked at her plate and didn't say anything.

"He was very proud of you. It wasn't right for Lori to try to use you as a lever."

"No," said Sara, low, "it wasn't."

"A man has to do what he has to do—and a woman, if she loves him, has to let him do it."

Sara smiled slightly. "You're getting very profound, Grandpa."

Aronsen grunted. "I'm getting senile is what it is."

Sara's smile widened. "No, you're not. And I'm so glad you invited me here. I'm having a wonderful time."

He looked at her for a moment in silence. Then he said, "I'm glad to have you, Sara. It's nice to have a granddaughter around the house."

*

Sara enjoyed helping Daniel out on the farm, but she found herself wishing more and more that they could just go out alone together, like any normal young couple. She understood, however, without Daniel ever having to put it in words, that he would never ask her out to dinner and dancing like B.J. and the other young men she knew. B.J. had once said that Daniel could date dozens of girls in Lexington—but Sara knew that she did not figure in that number; at least not in Daniel's eyes. It was not that he was humble; rather it was that he was too proud.

She and Daniel were leaning along a paddock fence one morning, watching the horses play and talking idly to each other, when there came the sound of a car from the road. They both turned instinctively to look. It was John Scott's small truck, and when he saw them he pulled over and got out.

Sara felt herself stiffening as she watched the vet come across the grass toward them. She acknowledged his greeting distantly and turned back to watch the horses as the two men talked.

"I understand you've been helping Daniel with the yearlings, Miss Underwood," Dr. Scott said to her after a few minutes.

Sara swung her chin in the vet's direction. "Yes. Well, he's let me think I'm helping, at any rate."

"How's B.J.? I haven't seen him in a while."

Sara's chin elevated a quarter of an inch. "He's very well, thank you."

The doctor gave her a narrow-eyed look before he turned back to Daniel. "Jane told me to invite you for dinner this week. Can you make it?"

Daniel sighed. "Does she have another nice girl for me to meet?"

"Probably. There's something about you, Daniel, that brings out her matchmaking instincts."

"It's very kind of her, John, but I can't come this week."

The vet's eyes went from Daniel's face to Sara's. "I see," he said. "Jane will be disappointed."

"Jane and who else?" Daniel asked humorously.

Dr. Scott smiled. "I think it's one of the Jordan girls this time." He clapped Daniel on the shoulder. "I'll get her to invite you for some home cooking without the trimmings."

"Thank you," Daniel said.

The vet nodded to Sara, "Miss Underwood," and said good-bye to Daniel. As he drove away down the road, Daniel turned to look at her.

"You can put your chin down now, girl. He's gone."

Sara didn't look at him. "He doesn't like me," she said flatly. "I always freeze up with people who don't like me."

"He doesn't like you because he's afraid you're going to get me into trouble with your grandfather."

Sara stared straight ahead. "Grandfather knows I've been helping you with the yearlings."

"Does he, now?"

"Yes."

"And that's all there is to it, then? You helping me with the yearlings?"

Sara slowly turned her head and looked at the narrow, dark, beautifully modeled face of the man next to her. Even more slowly she shook her head. "No." Her voice was very low, almost a whisper. "No, that's not all there is to it."

She saw his nostrils flare. "It should be," Daniel said almost roughly, and once again she shook her head.

He turned to stare once more at the horses in the paddock. His profile looked set and stern. "I don't want to make trouble for you, Daniel," Sara said. "I would never want to do that."

"I know that, girl."

They both watched the horses in silence. Then Daniel said, "I have the afternoon off tomorrow. Would you like to go for a picnic?"

Sara's heart jolted once and then began to race. "Yes."

"There's a nice little spot I know of a few miles from here. A little pond where there's usually no one around. I often spend an afternoon there."

Sara ran her tongue around her lips. "Do you want me to meet you there?"

He looked at her. "Yes."

"All right," she said. "Give me the directions."

*

When Sara pulled off the road the following afternoon, she saw Daniel's motorcycle hidden among the bushes. She turned the engine off, picked up her canvas bag containing a towel, lunch, and a thermos of juice, and went in among the woods toward the sparkle of water she could see through the trees.

Daniel was there already, sitting on a small filled-in strip of sand, throwing sticks for his dogs to fetch. He was wearing his usual uniform of jeans and knit shirt, but he was barefoot. As she came up to him, he took a stick from Deirdre, said, "Good girl," and looked up at Sara.

"Hi," she said.

"Hi," he returned gravely.

Sara put down her bag and looked around. "This is a super spot. How did you find it?"

"B.J. showed it to me. It's on Debrett land—his grandpa had the sand trucked in many years ago. B.J. called it a swimming hole."

Daniel was sitting on an old army blanket and now Sara dropped down gracefully beside him. She was wearing running shorts and a T-shirt over her bathing suit and she drew her long bare legs up, linking her arms around her knees.

"Does B.J. come here too?"

"No. They have the swimming pool now. But he felt sorry for the poor Irishman sweltering in the Kentucky summer two years ago and turned his pond over to me."

"That was nice of him." Sara rested her chin on her knees.

"He's a grand fellow, B.J. Debrett."

Fergus ran out from the woods where he had been chasing a squirrel and came over to greet Sara. She scratched behind his ears and smiled sideways at Daniel.

"I know," she said softly. "I like B.J. too."

He leaned back on his elbow and regarded her for a moment in silence. Sara sat quietly petting the dog.

"B.J. more than likes you, Sara."

She turned her head and looked directly at him. "Are you worrying about B.J.?"

His eyes were inscrutable, but as she spoke, laughter lines gathered at the corners of them.

"B.J.'s a big lad now," he answered her after a minute. "He can look out for his own interests."

Their eyes held for a minute and then Sara said briskly, "I thought we came here to swim. You can sit here in the sun if you like, but I'm going in the water." She stripped her T-shirt off over her head and began to unlace her sneakers. Daniel got to his feet, and when Sara looked up at him, his shirt was off and he was unbuckling the belt of his jeans. Sara stood up to take off her own shorts, feeling a little self-conscious. But with his usual deep delicacy, Daniel finished undressing and walked down to the water's edge without even glancing at her. Sara followed him slowly, her eyes on his back. Stripped to a pair of bathing trunks, he looked deeply tanned and hard as nails. He glanced over his shoulder at her. "Do you not be expecting any fancy swimming from me. I keep my head above water is all."

Sara stood beside him. "Isn't there much swimming in Ireland?"

"Sure, we have beaches and all, but it never gets that hot."

"I lived in England for a while when I was a little girl. I expect the climates are similar."

"They are. What were you doing in England?"

"Mother's second husband was English. He had a big house in Kent, and I lived there. I liked it, but then Mother got a divorce and we moved to Switzerland for a while."

Nothing could conceal from Daniel the loneliness evoked by this simple statement. He wanted to reach out and gather Sara close. He looked down at her profile, at the bare flesh of throat and shoulder so close to him. Her skin had the perfection and resilience of a baby's. He could not possibly touch her.

"Well, now," he said, "are you going in or not?"

She glanced up at him with a quick flashing smile. "I'm going in." She took four steps out into the pond and dived. After a minute Daniel followed.

*

They swam for a while and then they sat on the blanket and ate the lunch Sara had brought. It gave her such pleasure, to fix him a sandwich and pour him some of the juice. It was so quiet and peaceful, just the two of them.

"I can tell you're not an American just by the fact that you didn't bring a radio," Sara said as she packed the remnants of their lunch back into her canvas bag.

Daniel stretched out on his back, put his hands behind his head, and narrowed his eyes against the sky. "Some people can't stay quiet long enough to hear the birds sing," he said comfortably.

"It's true. We're surrounded by noise all the time. There's no peace anywhere."

"Horses are peaceful. There's nothing like coming into the barn early in the morning and hearing only the sounds of their feet moving around in the stalls and their teeth munching the hay."

"You really love horses, don't you?" Sara asked softly.

"I've spent my whole life around them. There are worse ways to live."

"Did your family have a farm?"

"My father worked for the Earl of Clonmel, ran his stable of hunters. He put me on a horse before I could even walk."

"Oh." Sara stretched out on her stomach next to him. She had longed to know something of his background, but he so seldom spoke of his life before coming to America. "Do you have sisters and brothers?" she asked.

"Two sisters—both older. They're married now. Olwen lives in Dublin, and Mary is in London. My mother and father are dead."

And you're planning to go back to Ireland?"

"Yes." He turned his head slightly to look at her. Their faces were very close. "My dad left me a piece of property in Tipperary. He saved all his life to buy it. It's a grand property—perfect for horses. I'm going to start a small stud and training stable for jumpers."

"It sounds lovely." She smiled at him a little wistfully

"It won't be an easy life." His voice did not sound quite normal to his own ears. "Not anything like Canfield."

Her eyes were absolutely golden. He had never seen anything like them. "It still sounds lovely," she said. She had a mouth that could drive a man mad, he thought suddenly.

"I think so." He could feel all his muscles tensing. "Sara, darlin', I don't think this picnic was such a good idea."

Her eyes widened slightly, the wide sulky mouth quivered. "Why?"

He reached his hand over and rested it lightly on the tender skin of her neck, under her pulled-back hair. "You know why," he said softly.

She didn't answer, but after a minute leaned over and touched her lips first to his temple and then to the black hair that had fallen forward across his forehead. The beautiful curve of her breast was so close to his mouth ... Daniel shuddered. Closing his eyes, he drew her face down to his and kissed her warm, inviting mouth. The kiss was long and sweeter than either of them could have imagined. Sara trembled and grasped Daniel's sun-bronzed shoulder, marveling at the feel of his lips against her own.

Suddenly Daniel circled her arm with his hand and put her away from him, sitting up abruptly. "Listen to me, my lovely one," he said almost sharply, "we are playing with fire, we two alone here together."

"I don't mind."

"Well, I do." He stood up and reached for his shirt. "We're leaving," he said. "Now." And he whistled for his dogs.

Sara obediently put on her own shirt and bent for her shoes. Unseen by him, there was a very faint smile on her lips. "All right, Daniel," she said. "Whatever you want." And she began to lace up her sneakers.

Chapter 8

It was raining. Daniel lay awake listening to the sound of the rain drumming on the roof of his cottage. It had been raining for hours—half the night—and for half the night he had been awake and listening.

He could not exorcise the tension from his body. He could not banish Sara from his mind. And so here he was awake, nor was there much likelihood of sleep in the near future.

Daniel was in what was for him an unusual situation. When he was sixteen years old the wife of one of the earl's guests had taught him what sex was all about, and since that time he had gathered a good deal of experience, but none of it had prepared him to cope with Sara.

He wasn't used to courtship. He wasn't used to holding hands and kissing. He had always steered clear of girls his own age—he wasn't ready to tie himself down with a family and he hadn't wanted to raise any false expectations.

When he had kissed a woman before, it had always been a prelude to the complete act. He had wanted very badly to go on kissing Sara this afternoon, but he had been desperately afraid he wouldn't be able to stop. He wanted her. He couldn't ever remember wanting like this before. And the more he saw of her, the worse it became.

She was attracted to him too. She had made that clear enough. They were both of age and of full mental competence. There was nothing to stop them from doing what both of them wanted to do.

And yet... Alongside his carnal passion for Sara there bloomed the softer emotions of protectiveness and care. She was so very vulnerable. When she put her lovely little chin in the air and her face took on its cool and remote *noli me tangere* look, he always wanted to gather her close into his arms and tell her not to worry, that no one would hurt her, that he wouldn't allow anyone to hurt her.

He could hardly be the one to hurt her himself.

He wondered if perhaps she had had an unhappy love affair. She was certainly wary of men—he could see that. But she wasn't wary of him. She would let him…

Daniel groaned and rolled over in bed. He had to stop thinking about her. And he had to stop seeing her.

He finally went to sleep and dreamed he was making love to her in a field of flowers.

*

Sara lay awake and listened to the sound of the rain drumming against her window. The smell of the night air drifted into her room—cool, fresh, and fragrant. She lay curled on her side and thought of Daniel.

There had never been anyone else like him. There never would be. Deep in Sara's soul—it was the deepest thing there—lay a belief that if the right man came along she could give herself completely.

Daniel was the right man. Sara felt that with utter certitude. In his arms she would find a home.

But she knew he was uneasy. She thought he was worried about the social and financial gap between them, the gap that would necessarily lie between a girl bred to luxury and fortune and a poor young trainer in her grandfather's stable.

It didn't concern Sara at all. She had to make him see that. It was not what he had, but what he was, that mattered.

She finally fell asleep and dreamed she was chasing him through a long dark hallway. Then her grandfather appeared and told her Daniel was dead. She woke up at dawn in a cold sweat.

*

At breakfast William Aronsen commented on Sara's pallor.

"I didn't sleep well," she confessed. "The rain kept me awake."

He grunted. "At your age, nothing should keep you awake."

"Youth is not a cure for all problems, Grandpa," Sara said with dignity.

He chuckled. "I suppose not." He looked at her appraisingly across the table. "Why don't you go back to bed if you're tired? Running around in the heat with Daniel all morning will only tucker you out more."

Sara shrugged. "I'm okay."

"We got an invitation to the Debretts' for dinner next week."

"Oh?" Sara raised an eyebrow. "When did that come?"

"Kay called yesterday."

"How nice," said Sara.

"I thought you liked B.J.," Aronsen said after a minute. "I'm not trying to push him down your throat, honey."

"Of course I like B.J., Grandpa. How could anyone not like B.J.? But you're right, I don't want him pushed down my throat."

"Fair enough," he said mildly. "Do you want me to cancel the dinner?"

"Of course not. I'll be happy to go to dinner, Grandpa. Just don't expect an engagement announcement, that's all."

"Fair enough," he repeated. "Fair enough."

*

Daniel had progressed to riding the yearlings in a small paddock and he was working one of the youngsters later in the morning when Sara came up alongside the paddock fence. Henry Gordon was already leaning against the fence, watching.

"Good morning, Sara," he said cordially as she came up beside him. He squinted a little at her in the bright sun. "That was some rain last night, wasn't it? Just what the grass needed."

Sara smiled. "Yes. It's lovely this morning." She watched Daniel in silence for a few minutes. He was cantering the youngster quietly around the paddock.

"Are you here to look over next year's prospects?" she asked Henry, her eyes still on Daniel.

"Yep. The Keeneland sales are the end of July, and we have to decide which yearlings we want to keep and which we want to sell."

"I see. I've never been to a horse sale. What's it like?"

"You'll have to come along to Keeneland and see for yourself," Henry replied.

He was still telling her about the sale when Daniel dismounted and led the horse over to where they were standing.

"He has a nice action, that one," Henry said.

"Yes. He should have—with his breeding."

"True. I'm meeting Seth Daniels over at Windfall Farms this afternoon. Do you want to come along, Daniel?"

"Surely," Daniel answered instantly. "I'd like that, Henry."

"Good. I'll pick you up at two. So long, Sara." The trainer smiled at her and walked over to his car, which was parked on the road.

"Do you want to open that gate for me, girl?" Daniel asked, and Sara silently went to do as he requested.

They walked the yearling back to the barn in silence. Glancing at Daniel from under her lashes, Sara thought he looked pale under his tan.

"Are you through riding for the morning?" she asked as they reached the barn.

He shook his head. "I've still one or two to do."

"Oh. Well, I'm no help to you with this sort of work. My own riding hasn't progressed far enough to put me on a yearling, that I do realize. I'll get out of your way, then. Perhaps I'll see you later."

She gave him a smile and turned to walk out of the barn.

"Sara..." His voice sounded strained. "What are you going to do this afternoon?"

She could have told him she was going swimming with B.J. or playing tennis with David, but the thought of trying to make him jealous never once crossed Sara's mind. She smiled again and said lightly, "I'm going to practice my own riding. I have a date with a mare named Lady."

After a minute his own rare smile dawned. "Watch out for bees," he said.

"I will." She turned and walked out once more into the sunshine.

*

Ten days went by. Sara saw Daniel around the farm but he made no mention of their meeting alone again. Nor did Sara bring up the subject. She spent what time she could with him and didn't press him for anything more.

With absolute innocence, Sara was doing the one thing that would infallibly lead Daniel on. Until now he had always been the one pursued. It had always been his beauty that was the sought-after object of another's desire. Daniel consequently had almost a reflex action against being chased. With perfect and complete courtesy, he could put up a No Trespassing sign that was absolutely unmistakable. He had learned from early manhood how to protect himself against predators.

With Sara his usual position was reversed, and it was he who was the pursuer. Even in the days when she had first arrived and was following him about like a puppy dog, he had known that it was she who was the vulnerable one. She was so very sweet, so soft and tender, so easily hurt. She would yield like silken ribbons under his touch.

He knew he should leave her alone. Her wealth and his poverty were a chasm that would always lie between them. He did not think it mattered to Sara, but he knew it mattered to him. "Fortune hunter" was an ugly title, one his pride could never tolerate.

He would leave her alone. Never again would he put himself in the tempting situation he had created the other afternoon. An occasion of sin, the church called it; the church was right. The sight of Sara in a bathing suit had nearly undone him.

Best to leave things as they were. Best to remain only friends.

If only he could get a decent night's sleep.

*

Sara appeared to be perfectly content to remain just friends. She helped him around the farm when she could, and when he was busy with others, she tactfully disappeared. B.J. was giving her jumping lessons, she told him. It seemed to Daniel that she spent most of her afternoons over at Inverlochy.

Sara was, in fact, seeing quite a lot of B.J., but her motives were scarcely romantic. She wanted to learn to ride better, because she liked it and because Daniel rode so well. B.J. was merely a means to an end, and as long as he was willing to teach her, Sara was willing to learn. She went out of her way to show B.J. that her regard for him was only friendship.

That feeling of friendship was genuine, however, and she went out to dinner and parties with him gladly. But on one particular night, at an especially tiresome barbecue, Sara excused herself early, saying she had a headache, and left by herself.

She was driving the silver-gray coupe her grandfather had put at her disposal and she cruised toward home without any trouble until she reached the gates of Canfield Farm. She put her foot on the brake to slow down for the turn, and the engine suddenly died.

Sara frowned and tried to start it up again. Nothing happened. The car had rolled inside the farm gates and so was safely off the road. Sara picked up her purse, locked the car, and started to walk the two miles or so to the house.

The farm road was very dark, and the mosquitoes were out in full force. Sara trudged along determinedly, grateful that at least she was not wearing high heels.

The lights of Daniel's cottage gleamed a little ahead of her on the right. Sara stared at the lit windows with longing. She could stop, and Daniel would take her the rest of the way home on his motorcycle.

Should she do it?

Unconsciously her steps slowed as she came abreast of the small white house. She hesitated, and suddenly there came the sound of the dogs barking.

"Fergus. Deirdre." Sara spoke softly but firmly. "Hush. It's only me."

The door of the cottage opened and there, framed in the light, stood Daniel.

"Who is there?" he asked. His voice did not sound friendly.

"It's me, Daniel. Sara."

"Sara?" He came out onto the front steps. "What are you doing here?"

The dogs had stopped barking. "My car broke down at the gate. I'm walking home."

"In the dark? By yourself?"

"I didn't have much choice. The car won't start up."

The light from the porch lamp was shining directly on his face. "Come in for a minute." There was a trace of impatience in his voice. "The mosquitoes are all getting into the house."

Sara went up the path to the house with the dogs following her. They all went in together through the front door.

Daniel closed it behind them.

The dogs padded over to the iron stove in the living room and stretched out in what were clearly their accustomed places. Sara looked around the small room. A lamp was lit on one of the maple end tables and a magazine lay carelessly open on the chintz-covered sofa. He had been reading before the barking had brought him outside. She looked at him gravely and didn't speak.

"Where were you?" he asked abruptly.

"At a party at Dawn's. I left early and drove myself home. The car was going fine until it stalled at the gates. I couldn't get it going again."

"I'll run you the rest of the way home on my motorbike if you like."

"Thank you, Daniel. That would be great. The mosquitoes were feasting on me."

"Would you like a cup of coffee first?" He hadn't meant to say it, but it was out before he could think.

She smiled slightly. "Thanks, yes."

He turned and went into the kitchen, Sara following. The kitchen was a middle-size room containing an elderly-looking refrigerator and stove, a Formica table, and four chairs. Sara sat in one of the chairs. Daniel went to the stove and lit the burner under the kettle.

"It's early," he said to her over his shoulder. "Not even eleven. Why were you after leaving your party?"

Sara shrugged slim bare shoulders. "Boredom, I suppose."

"Ah." He turned to face her, blue eyes brilliant in his dark face. "Boredom. The malaise of the rich."

Sara put her elbows on the table and rested her chin on her linked hands. "Mm," she said. "I know. Hardworking proletariat types like you never have time to get bored."

"That's right."

"If you'll lend me a handkerchief, I'll cry."

He gave her one of his rare, quick, schoolboy smiles. "No need for that, girl. I don't want your tears." The kettle began to whistle. "Instant coffee or tea?" he asked.

"Tea, please." She watched as he got out cups and saucers and tea bags. "Do you cook for yourself?" she asked curiously.

"Breakfast I do." He brought the cups over to the table. "Dinner I eat with the rest of the boys. I'm not too handy in the kitchen."

"Neither am I," Sara confessed as she poured milk into her tea.

She looked up to find him watching her, a look of faint amusement on his face. "You never had the opportunity," he said. His knit shirt was unbuttoned at the throat and the overhead kitchen light played against the bones of his face.

"Nor the desire," she replied honestly.

He smiled again, and the hollows of his cheek deepened and the light played still more beautifully against his features. "Who was at this party?" he asked.

She gazed at him, oblivious of her cooling tea. "The usual crowd."

"B.J.?"

"Yes, B.J. was there."

"Why didn't he take you home?"

Daniel appeared to have forgotten his tea as well. Their voices were quiet, intimate. Inside the living room, one of the dogs began to snore.

"I didn't want him to," Sara said. "That's why I drove myself, so no one would have to take me home."

Daniel went to pick up his tea and then, abruptly, he put it down again. "Sara, darlin'," he said, "this isn't going to work. Not the two of us. It just won't work."

Sara picked up a napkin from the table and began to fold it. After a minute she looked up at him. "Why not?" she asked simply. "Tell me, Daniel. Why not...?"

Chapter 9

Daniel drew in a deep, shaken breath, stood up, and went over to the sink. "I don't have to tell you that," he said almost roughly. "It's obvious, I should think."

"It's not obvious to me. Is it that you're afraid for your job?"

"No." Now he sounded angry. "I'm almost finished with the job anyway. I'll be on my way back to Ireland soon."

Sara bent her head so that her loose hair swung forward, making a screen for her face. "Oh," she said in a very small voice.

He stared at her for a moment. The sound of crickets humming came from outside the windows, and from the living room, the rumble of his dogs snoring. He stared at the tender white nape exposed by Sara's parted hair. He could almost feel the smooth flesh of it in his hands. He imagined what her body would feel like under his in bed....

He shook his head as if to clear it. What had he been saying? "I'm going to buy some horses before I go home. Henry's been helping me look about."

Sara raised her head very slowly. "I see." Her voice was quiet. She stood up carefully. "Well, then, perhaps you can give me that motorbike ride home."

Her face had assumed its familiar guarded look. All of a sudden he felt he could not bear to see her look that way. "Don't you see what you are doing to me?" His voice was almost desperate. "I'm not like B.J., Sara. I can't be satisfied with just a few kisses. I should not have asked you in here. We should not be alone here together. It isn't safe...."

His voice broke off as Sara turned to him, her face suddenly illuminated. She crossed the room slowly until she stood before him, and then, with the simple trust of a child, she laid her cheek on his shoulder.

"I'm always safe," she said, her voice a little muffled, "if I'm with you."

Without any volition on his part his hand came up to caress her hair. It was like silk. He curved his fingers around the nape of her neck. It felt fragile to him; *she* was so fragile. His hand slid along the line of her jaw to her chin and tilted her head up. Then he kissed her.

This time her mouth was like honey, opening immediately under the pressure of his, yielding, responding, telling him without words that whatever he wanted of her, he could have.

"Sara. Love." His voice was almost a croak and his mouth moved over her face, kissing her eyelids, her cheeks, then coming back once again to that tantalizing mouth. She was arched up against him, her slender body taut and trembling. He slid a hand beneath the fabric of her bodice and touched her breast. It was as silky and smooth as the rest of her. He felt her nipple stand up hard against the palm of his hand, and he groaned.

"Do you want to go into the bedroom?" she whispered.

Did he want to…? He tried to regain his self-control but it was fast slipping away. She stepped back from him a little and gazed up into his face. Her eyes looked heavy-lidded and purely golden. Her mouth was a little swollen from his kisses. God, that mouth… He didn't speak, just put his hand on her arm and led her into his bedroom.

He was consumed as if by a torrent. With others there had always been time for thought, time for skill, time to savor the prospect of physical satisfaction. With Sara there was only need, only this torrent driving him forward, catching her up in the violence of its rush and carrying her along. It was not until he heard her cry out that he realized she was a virgin.

She lay nestled quietly in his arms and he felt his heart would break with love for her. She was his. She had never been anyone else's. "I hurt you," he said. "I didn't know. You should have told me."

But she was shaking her head in denial. "No, Daniel. You didn't hurt me. Really you didn't."

He held her close against him and he knew the course of his life had changed, like a river that bends its direction when it meets with a great natural obstacle. Nothing would ever be the same now that he had held this precious one, this vulnerable one, this beloved one in his arms.

She stirred against him and kissed his collarbone. "I love you, Daniel," she breathed.

His hand moved caressingly in her hair, smoothing it back from her hot forehead. "Is it so?" he asked softly. And under his hand her head nodded in affirmation.

*

It was after two when he finally took her home on his motorcycle. She kissed his cheek swiftly before she ran up the stairs and let herself into the house. She stayed perfectly still behind the closed door until she heard the motorcycle rev up and take off down the drive. Then she went quietly up the stairs to her room. She undressed slowly and stood for a minute in front of the full-length mirror, staring in wonder at her naked body. Daniel thought she was beautiful. She closed her eyes for a moment, imagining the feel of his hands on her flesh. She opened her eyes, smiled a little guiltily at her reflection, and went into the bathroom to shower.

When she got into bed, lying on top of the cool sheet with only another sheet over her, she curled on her side and stared into the darkness, thinking.

Daniel. Never had she imagined she could be this happy. She did not think of the future, she thought only of the joy of being at last in Daniel's arms. Love, he had called her. My darling girl.

She drifted off to sleep, peaceful as a baby.

*

The following day was Daniel's afternoon off and when he saw Sara in the morning he quickly made arrangements for them to meet over at B.J.'s swimming hole. Sara went home to call B.J. and cancel her riding lesson and to ask the cook to pack her a lunch.

"Where are you going, Sara?" her grandfather asked when he ran into her on the front steps. "I thought you were having a riding lesson with B.J."

"Oh, it's too hot, Grandpa," Sara replied quickly. "We decided to go for a picnic instead."

"Mmph," Aronsen grunted. "Where you picnicking, then?"

"I'm not sure, Grandpa. Someplace B.J. knows."

"Well, have fun, honey."

Sara gave her grandfather a radiant smile. "I will," she promised, and scooted down the stairs. The gray coupe which had given her trouble the night before had been jump-started by a farmworker and appeared to be in operating condition. She got in now and drove off, watched all the way by William Aronsen's assessing eyes.

*

Sara was first at the swimming hole this time. She carried her lunch and her blanket carefully down the path and settled herself on the tiny beach. She took off her sneakers and shirt but left her shorts on over her jade-green maillot bathing suit. She propped her chin on her knees and stared dreamily out at the water.

Daniel arrived fifteen minutes later. He dropped down beside her and stretched out comfortably on the blanket, leaning up on one elbow. A lock of soot-black hair had fallen forward over his forehead and Sara reached out with a maternal gesture to smooth it back. He smiled at her faintly, amusement in his blue eyes.

"I see your car is working again," he said.

"Yes. Frank thinks I probably flooded it last night." She gave him a mischievous look. "I must say I'm glad I did."

He picked up her hand and held it in a light clasp. "Are you, girl?"

The mischievous look left Sara's face. "Yes. I am."

He moved her hand to his mouth. "They're chancy things, cars. I'll take a horse any day."

His lips were on her palm. Sara half-closed her eyes. "You can't exactly ride a horse into Lexington," she murmured.

"More's the pity." His lips moved to her wrist. "Sara ..." he said. Her pulse was racing under his touch. He reached up and pulled her down beside him, holding her close along the length of his body.

"Last night," he said into her ear, "I could not help myself. I hurt you ..."

Sara closed her eyes. The sweet smell of honeysuckle was heavy in the air and she felt a corresponding warm heavy sweetness swelling deep inside her. She slid her hands down his back, feeling the hardness of muscle under the warm cotton fabric. He kissed her lightly on the temple.

"Oh dear," she said, and there was a husky, throbbing note in her voice. "Does that mean you *can* help yourself now?"

"God. Sara." His voice was husky as well. "You are so sweet." And he kissed her again, not quickly this time, but long and slow.

Sara's arms came up to encircle him, and after a minute she arched her back, lifting her body so he could pull the bathing suit and shorts off her and toss them aside. He knelt for a minute to strip off his own clothing; then he was back beside her once more with no foreign fabric to get in their way.

The hot afternoon shook and then burst into flames of wildfire. Sara was blind and dumb and all there was of her was this raging fire that Daniel's hands were stoking and stoking....

She could do nothing for herself. She let herself be helpless, wanting only for him to enter her, to fill her, to fulfill her.

He said her name and then he drove into her and the whole world seemed to explode.

A long time later he was lying with his face against the hollow of her throat. Sara looked up at the sky through half-closed eyes and let her fingers slip caressingly through his thick black hair. She looked down the length of the two of them. His skin looked so dark against hers.

"I don't ever want to move," she said softly. "I'd like to stay here forever, just the two of us. We could pretend we were in the forest of Arden, like Orlando and Rosalind. Wouldn't that be lovely?"

"Even Orlando and Rosalind had to leave the forest and return to the real world, if I remember rightly." Reluctantly he raised his head. "Girl, dear, you're a wonder." He kissed the curve of her jaw and sat up.

Sara didn't move. "This is the real world."

"Love of my soul," he said, "it isn't."

She lay where she was and watched him. His face had taken on a grave and remote look and she felt suddenly frightened.

"I don't want the real world, then," she said childishly. "I want this."

His face did not lighten, nor did he look at her. "Do you not be so foolish," he said.

"I'm not foolish." She sat up and leaned toward him, her long hair tumbling around her shoulders, her golden eyes dark and troubled. "What's the matter, Daniel? Why have you suddenly ... gone away?"

"I did not mean to go away." He turned to look at her. "Nor can I conduct a discussion with you sitting here beside me naked. Get yourself dressed, girl." His voice was mockingly severe, and Sara smiled in relief.

"Oh, can't you?" she said. "Then you can hand me the garments you so ruthlessly discarded earlier."

He picked up her bathing suit and threw it to her. "Not that it's much, but it's better than nothing at all," he murmured.

"I have a sweatshirt in my bag," Sara said demurely.

"Away with you," he said. "The bathing suit will do fine." And he reached for his own trunks.

"Let's walk," he said when they both were once again clothed. "I can't think unless I'm in motion." He rose to his feet with effortless grace and held out a hand to her. "I think best on horseback," he added.

"I know what you mean," Sara said. She let him pull her to her feet. "I do a lot of thinking when I'm driving."

He kept her hand in his and started to walk around the edge of the pond toward a wide path that cut from the water and through the woods to the north.

"That doesn't sound a very safe place for thinking, girl," he said. "When you're driving you should be watching where you're going, not thinking of something else."

"Well, I could say the same thing about you on horseback," Sara returned defensively.

He shook his head. "Oh no. A horse is a living creature, with eyes and a brain of his own. A car is a machine. There's no comparison between the two."

"You don't sound as if you much like cars, Daniel," Sara said curiously.

He smiled faintly. "They're a necessary nuisance, I suppose."

"A motorcycle is far more dangerous than a car," Sara pointed out.

"True. It's also cheaper."

"I guess." They veered off into the path through the woods. "What did you want to think about?" she asked softly after they had walked in silence for a few minutes.

He was looking ahead and frowning slightly. "You," he said. "And me."

"Oh." Sara felt a sudden chill of apprehension.

"I told you I was going back to Ireland. In fact, I made a bid on two mares of Harold Price's the other afternoon to take back with me. The barns are built. I've finally got the money to start up on my own."

"Ow!" Sara halted abruptly, tears stinging her eyes.

"What happened?" He turned to her in quick concern.

"I stepped on a rock. This path is too rough for me, Daniel. I didn't put my sneakers on."

He didn't say anything for a minute, just stood there looking at her. Then, "Poor little girl. I was not even looking. Come along with you back to the sand, where you won't be bruising your tender feet."

They began to walk slowly back toward the water. "I love you, Daniel," Sara said softly. "I love you so very much."

"I know you do, darlin'," he returned very soberly, "but I'm thinking that my path will always be too rough for you."

"I wouldn't care how rough the path, so long as I could be with you." Her mouth trembled a little. "That is, if you want me."

He lifted his eyes suddenly. "Want you? With you at my side, I'd be like a king wearing his crown. But the life of a farmer's wife is hard. Very hard. It's not the life for the likes of Sara Underwood."

He had mentioned marriage. Sara's heart soared and she put a hand on his forearm. "But, Daniel, I love farm life. I've been happier here at Canfield than I've ever been in my whole life!"

"Canfield is nothing at all like my farm in Ireland." There was a note of suppressed violence in his voice. "Your grandfather lives here like a prince—aye, and you like a princess, Sara. There would be no one to wait on you in Ireland." They came out from the shelter of the trees into the sunshine. "I'm a poor man, girl. I can offer you nothing like the life you are accustomed to."

"The life I'm accustomed to is damnably lonely."

He reached for her wrist and pulled her close. "I know," he murmured against her hair. "But I want you to be sure. I'm not one for divorce, you know."

Sara heaved a heart-shattering sigh. "Oh, Daniel, neither am I."

He cradled her against him and Sara closed her eyes. "I wasn't planning to leave until September," he said. "We have a little time before we need to decide anything."

"Mm." So long as she could be with him, could feel his arms around her like this, Sara knew she would be happy. In a month she could surely convince him to take her back to Ireland with him. "I love you," she said again, and he bent his head and began to kiss her.

Chapter 10

Sara went home, flushed with sunshine and love. Daniel wanted to marry her. She had only to convince him that money didn't matter to her. And it didn't—she was sublimely confident of that. She had had money all her life, but she had never been happy until she found Daniel.

Sara went in the front door of the house and started up the stairs to shower and change for dinner. "'I know where I'm going,'" she sang as she went:

I know who's going with me,
I know who I love,
But the dear knows who I'll marry.

She ought to make a recording of that song and send it to Daniel, she thought.

I have stockings of silk
Shoes of fine green leather,
Combs to buckle my hair
And a ring for every finger.

She reached the top of the stairs, and grasping the banister in one hand, executed a very creditable arabesque.

Feather beds are soft,
Painted rooms are bonny,
But I'd leave them all
To go with my love Johnny.

Sara did a series of chenées down the hall.

Some say he's black,
I say he's bonny
He's the flower of them all
My handsome, winsome Johnny.

She closed the door of her bedroom behind her.

I know where I'm going,
I know who's going with me,
I know who I love,
But the dear knows who I'll marry.

There was the sound of a car on the drive and Sara went to the window. B.J.'s sports car had just pulled up and she could see B.J. getting out.

"Good God," said Sara, and raced out of her room and down the stairs. She had told her grandfather she was picnicking with B.J. that afternoon. William Aronsen was greeting B.J. as Sara arrived in the front hall.

"Well, that was quick," Sara's grandfather was saying jovially to an obviously bewildered B.J. "I see your car has been repaired, B.J."

"My car?" said BJ. blankly.

"Hi, B.J.," Sara said enthusiastically. "Is that the record you promised to lend me?"

"Yes." B.J. slightly raised the album he held in his hand.

"Come on into the den for a minute," Sara urged, "and I'll put it on."

"Okay," said B.J.

"I hope you enjoyed your picnic this afternoon," Aronsen said cordially.

Sara stiffened. After a brief pause B J. replied, "It was very enjoyable, sir, thank you." He turned and followed Sara into the den.

B.J. closed the door and stood staring at her, the record in his hand.

Sara could feel the color coming into her cheeks. "I'm sorry. B.J.," she said, "I did tell Grandpa I was going on a picnic with you this afternoon."

He looked at her, his back still to the door. She had not had time to change her clothes. "Who did you go on a picnic with, Sara?" When she didn't answer, he went on, "Was it Daniel?"

Sara raised her chin. "Yes," she said defiantly, looking him in the eye.

He didn't answer but advanced a little into the room. "Daniel," he repeated, and put the record down on the sofa. "So you've been seeing Daniel." His voice sounded flat.

"Yes," said Sara, still defiantly. Then, when he didn't say anything, she asked, "How did you guess it was Daniel, B.J.?"

He didn't choose to answer her question, but asked another one instead. "Why are you keeping it from your grandfather?"

Sara sat down on the sofa abruptly. "Grandpa knows I've been helping Daniel with the yearlings. We...we haven't seen all that much of each other outside the farm. This afternoon, when I met him for a picnic...well, it just seemed easier to say it was you instead. I'm sorry, B.J."

B.J. sat down too. "Does Daniel know you lied to your grandfather?"

Sara flushed. "No."

"How serious is this, Sara?" She didn't answer and he went on steadily, "I think I have a right to know that."

Sara's mouth quivered and then set. "Daniel's going to leave for Ireland in September. I want us to be married so I can go back with him."

"*You* want. And what does Daniel want?"

"Oh..." Sara made an impatient gesture. "He's afraid the life will be too hard for me. But it won't. I know it won't."

She had turned a little toward him on the sofa. Her long slender legs in their Nike running shorts were a beautiful pale golden color. The sun slanting in the window drew coppery sparks from her hair. She looked at B.J. gravely and said, "I love him so much."

It never even crossed her mind that she was hurting him. B.J. knew that, knew that Sara was not being deliberately cruel. He drew in a deep, unsteady breath. "Have you ever done one day of hard physical labor in your life, Sara?" he asked.

Her wide golden eyes flew to his face. "No," she said in a low voice.

"Life in Ireland will be very different from life at Canfield. I know. I've been on some small Irish stud farms. It's damn hard work, let me tell you. It's mucking out stalls and pitching hay and grooming and cleaning and riding from before sunup till after sundown. That's what Daniel will be doing, Sara."

"Well," Sara said defensively, "that's what he does now."

B.J. laughed, and to his own ears the laugh was not a pleasant sound. "Oh no. Daniel's job here at Canfield is a vacation compared to what he's going to be doing in Ireland."

Sara was very pale now. "I don't care," she said. "All I care about is Daniel."

B.J. got to his feet. He frowned and looked down at her for a minute, then went over to the window and stared out. "You say you care about him. But do you *know* him, Sara?"

"Of course I know him!"

B.J. turned so his back was to the window. He ran a hand through his hair. "Then you know what a single-minded devil he is. He's perfectly capable of doing without the things you and I take for granted—companionship, recreation—Christ, I don't think he's bought himself a new shirt in two years!"

"He was saving his money for the farm."

"I know he was. That's just my point. And don't get me wrong—I admire Daniel. I probably admire him more than anyone else I know. But I couldn't live like that. And I don't think you can either."

Sara got to her feet. In her sneakers, running shorts, and T-shirt she didn't look any older than eighteen. "Yes, I can," she said stubbornly.

He shrugged. "All right. Maybe you can. But Daniel's Irish Catholic, Sara. If he marries you he's going to mean till death do us part."

There were two bright spots of color on her cheeks. "I'll mean it too."

"Well"—B.J. gestured helplessly toward the stereo—"there's your record."

"Thank you, B.J."

He walked slowly to the door of the den. "Will you be at the Jockey Club dance on Thursday?"

"Yes, I think so."

He nodded. "See you then."

"Good-bye, B.J."

She let him find his own way out and then went back upstairs to shower and change. But her joyful mood had gone.

Have you ever done one day of hard physical labor in your life?

Of course she hadn't. But she was young and strong. She could learn.

She had never even cooked a meal. Or cleaned a house. She had run a washing machine only one or two times in her life. There probably wasn't even a washing machine at Daniel's farm. There probably wasn't any electricity. Or central heating. Bathrooms? Surely there must be bathrooms.

Sara came out of the shower in a terry-cloth robe and went to look out the window in the direction of Daniel's cottage. B.J. was right, she thought. Daniel was perfectly capable of living without all of those things.

Was she?

Of course I am, Sara told herself firmly. If I'm with Daniel, I can cope with anything. And she resolutely refused to let herself think about what B.J. had said.

*

Four days later Lorraine arrived at Canfield. Sara came in at about four o'clock to find her mother and her grandfather having a drink on the patio.

"Mother!" Sara exclaimed in surprise.

"Hello, darling." Lorraine put down her drink and held up her cheek for Sara to kiss. "I thought I'd surprise you and Grandpa and come for a little visit."

"I thought you were in Capri."

"I was. Now I'm here."

"Well...it's good to see you, Mother."

"Thank you, darling," Lorraine replied tranquilly.

"Can I get you something to drink, Sara?" Aronsen asked.

"Thank you, Grandpa, but I think I'll go shower first."

"A very good idea, darling," Lorraine said firmly, surveying Sara's jeans and dusty shoes with distaste. "Whatever have you been doing?"

"Longeing horses," Sara replied cheerfully.

"With Daniel?" Aronsen asked blandly.

"Yes."

He nodded. "Well, go ahead and shower, honey. You can have your drink when you come back."

Sara flashed her grandfather a quick grin. "Okay, Grandpa."

As she left the room she could hear her mother asking, "Who is Daniel?"

*

Dinner that evening was a pleasant, relatively unstrained affair. Lorraine went out of her way to be charming, and she did have a great deal of charm when she chose to exert it. But all the time she chatted and laughed, her senses were closely attuned to her daughter.

Sara was different. There was a difference in the way she carried herself, in the awareness in her eyes; even the shape of her mouth seemed to have changed. She's got a lover, Lorraine thought. At last. I wonder who it is?

"Are you going out with B.J. tonight?" her grandfather asked Sara genially.

Sara shook her head. "No, not tonight, Grandpa. I'm staying home tonight."

"Who is B.J.?" asked Lorraine.

"B.J. Debrett—grandson of Ben Debrett, the fellow who has the farm down the road. He's been squiring Sara around ever since she got here."

"Debrett." Lorraine frowned. "There's a Debrett on Wall Street."

"B.J.'s father, Jimmy. He never was interested in horses."

Lorraine's eyes widened. "James Debrett's son. Very nice, Sara. Very nice indeed."

Sara flushed. "It's not like that, Mother. B.J. and I are just friends."

Lorraine smiled at Sara. "If you say so, darling."

"Come along with us to the Jockey Club dance, Lori, and you can meet all of Sara's friends."

"I'd love to," Lorraine replied instantly. "What kind of a dance is it, Dad?"

"It's put on by the local Jockey Club—*a* benefit affair. All funds go to the jockeys' pension fund. Everyone in Lexington will be there."

"Everyone?"

"Well, everyone connected with the horse business."

Sara grinned. "And in Lexington, Mother, that *is* everyone."

Lorraine smiled. "Is it formal? It's a good thing I brought a gown."

"Is BJ. taking you, Sara?" Aronsen asked.

"No." Sara smiled. "Actually, Grandpa, I'm going with you. If you don't mind, that is."

He returned her smile and his whole face lit with tenderness. "It will be my pleasure, honey," he said with old-fashioned courtesy.

Lorraine's eyes went from her father's face to her daughter's and then back to her father's. Her mouth thinned a little and her eyes narrowed at what she saw. It was a good thing she had come to Kentucky when she had, Lorraine thought. A very good thing.

Chapter 11

The night of the Jockey Club dance, Sara sat at her grandfather's table with Lorraine and William Aronsen's elderly friends. She wore a gown of pale-green silk and had arranged her hair up off her neck in a high knot of coppery ringlets. While the orchestra played, a succession of young men appeared at their table to ask Sara to dance. Lorraine was charming and had two millionaires hanging on her every word. But her attention was on her daughter.

B.J. Debrett brought Sara back to the table after their dance and sat down for a few minutes at Aronsen's invitation. Lorraine watched him speculatively: a handsome boy, a rich boy, but not the boy. Too bad, Lorraine thought as B.J. left the table with obvious reluctance. All that lovely money. Then she saw a slim, dark young man approaching.

"Good evening, sir," the newcomer said in a soft Irish voice to her father.

Aronsen smiled. "Daniel, boy, glad to see you here."

Lorraine's eyes were wide and startled as they took in that beautiful face. She heard Sara greet him and glanced quickly at her daughter.

"Mother," Sara said, "may I introduce Daniel Riordan."

"How do you do, Mrs. Burnett," Daniel murmured politely, and Lorraine extended her hand.

"How do you do," she replied in kind as her hand was briefly grasped by the thin, hard, ringless hand of her daughter's lover.

"Would you care to dance with me, Sara?" Daniel asked, and Sara rose instantly.

"Of course." She came around behind her grandfather's chair to stand next to Daniel. He took her arm with a gesture of perfect naturalness and Sara shot a quick sideways look at his profile. Then they moved off together onto the dance floor.

"Who was *that*?" Lorraine asked her father in a slightly awed voice.

Aronsen smiled. "That was one of my assistant trainers, Lori. He's a splendid boy."

Lorraine stared at her father in astonishment.

"Do you mean to tell me he's the farmworker Sara has been spending so much time with?"

Aronsen frowned slightly. "An assistant trainer, Lorraine, not a farmworker. There's a difference."

Lorraine made a dismissive gesture. "Dad, how could you be foolish enough to let a man like that loose around Sara? Don't you see what's going on? Didn't you see how she looked at him?"

"How did she look at him, Lori?" Aronsen asked tranquilly.

"As if she were bringing him gifts of gold and frankincense," Lorraine said grimly.

Aronsen's smile returned. "I gave up on B.J. weeks ago," he confided. "I've had a feeling all along that it was Daniel who beat him out. You think so too, eh?"

Lorraine compressed her lips and stared at her father.

"How about taking a turn with me on the dance floor, Mrs. Burnett?" the silver-haired gentleman on her right inquired. After a moment's hesitation, Lorraine acquiesced with a smile.

*

"You look very elegant in your tux," Sara murmured to Daniel as they danced to the orchestra's slow beat.

"Courtesy of the rental place in town," he returned.

"When did you get here? I've been looking for you for ages."

"I've been talking to Harold Price," he said.

They were directly under the chandelier now. "We finalized the deal for those mares."

"Daniel!" Sara smiled at him delightedly. Her skin was flawless, her eyes shone with health and happiness, her teeth were perfectly white and even. Her dress, Daniel found himself thinking, probably cost the price of one of his mares. He knew the strand of pearls she wore around her slender neck had to be real.

"I'm so glad," she was saying. "I know how much you wanted them."

"He's going to keep them for me until September." He was holding her lightly as they danced, and now he seemed to step away from her a little. "I'll be giving my notice to your grandfather in the morning," he said.

"Oh," said Sara. "I see."

They finished the dance in silence and when the music stopped Daniel said, "Come along with me out to the terrace."

The two of them disappeared from the ballroom, utterly unaware that their departure was closely observed by at least a half-dozen people.

They were alone on the country-club terrace and Daniel walked over to the stone balustrade and rested his hands on it lightly. "We've been busy as two bees avoiding this question, haven't we, girl?" he asked.

Sara nodded solemnly. She went and stood next to him. "Daniel," she said in a low voice, "take me with you."

"I want to." His mouth looked very rigid. "God knows how I want to. But when I look at you tonight..." He turned to her, his eyes shadowed. "My golden girl," he said softly, "with your beautiful little head sitting so proudly on your long lovely neck. How can I possibly take you with me, girl? How can I?"

"Oh, Daniel." Sara stepped closer to him and put her arms around his waist, holding him tightly. "I'm ignorant and useless—I know I am. But I love you. I love you so much."

"Hush." His own arms came up to hold her strongly. "Let you think about it," he said. "I'll give my notice tomorrow, but I want you to think some more. Then—if you're really certain—we can be married and go together."

Sara closed her eyes and snuggled her cheek into his shoulder. "I'm certain now."

"I could get someone in from the village to help you," he said. "The house is old, Sara. There are none of the modern conveniences you're accustomed to."

She could hear the doubt in his voice, and it was as if he were pouring acid on the corrosion of her insecurities. He didn't think she could do it. Neither did B.J. Maybe they were right. Maybe she wasn't competent... She couldn't bear it if he married her and then found her to be a burden.

The patio door openedm and she stepped away from Daniel. "Your mother sent me to hunt you out, Sara," B.J. said apologetically.

Sara's face closed. "Oh? Is she at the table, B.J.?"

"Yes."

"I'll go, then." She smiled quickly at Daniel and disappeared through the door, leaving the two men alone together on the terrace.

B.J. walked over to stand next to Daniel. "Harold Price was telling me you've bought two of his mares."

"Yes. I'll buy my stallion in Ireland, where it's cheaper, but I wanted to bring back some American thoroughbred mares."

"When are you leaving, then?"

"September. I'll be giving notice tomorrow."

Daniel leaned carelessly against the balustrade, looking as at home in his rented tuxedo as he did in his riding clothes.

"I wish you had left two months ago," B.J. said, and Daniel's eyes lifted to his face.

"I was not sure how serious you were," he replied slowly after a brief, tense pause. "Sara never said."

"Sara never knew." There was an unmistakable edge of bitterness in B.J.'s voice now. "She doesn't have a thought to spare for anyone but you. I don't think she even realizes the rest of us are flesh and blood."

Daniel's face did not lighten. "No." He stretched his back like an athlete who has been inactive for too long, then straightened up.

"Do you not be saying anything, B.J. We've not made any final decisions."

B.J. looked surprised. "Haven't you?"

"No," said Daniel uncompromisingly. "I think we'd best be getting back to the party." He stopped halfway across the patio and turned to look at B.J. "It should have been you," he said. "It would have been better so."

B.J. put a hand on Daniel's arm. "*She* wouldn't agree. Come on, fella, and I'll buy you a drink."

The party continued until after two. Sara was indefatigable, Daniel thought, watching her laugh at something one of her grandfather's friends had said. She fit so perfectly into this elegant and expensive scene. He realized he had never seen her in her natural surroundings until now.

"You didn't come on your motorcycle, did you?" she asked him as they danced the last dance together.

"No," he replied, thinking that she looked as flawless at two in the morning as she had looked at eight. "I came with Henry and Dot."

He was looking at her in such an odd way. Sara had a brief moment of intense fear, sensing that he was slipping away from her. "Daniel," she said with sudden intensity, "let's tell Grandpa we're going to get married. Let's tell him tomorrow when you give your notice."

A blue flame showed in his eyes. "I thought we had agreed to wait."

"But what's the point, Daniel? I'm not going to change my mind. Are you?"

"All right, then." The music stopped and they were left looking into each other's eyes. "We'll tell him tomorrow."

"Sara." It was her mother's silvery voice. "We're leaving now, darling."

"All right, Mother." Sara gave Daniel a quick, wistful smile and turned to Lorraine. Lorraine was looking at Daniel, and her expression was not friendly.

"Good night to you, Mrs. Burnett," Daniel said softly.

"Good night." And Lorraine put a hand on Sara's arm and almost pulled her away.

*

When Daniel arrived at the house the following morning, Sara was waiting for him.

"Grandpa is out on the terrace having breakfast," she told him. "Mother's not up yet."

He looked at her in faint amusement. "Are you coming with me?" He was wearing a white knit shirt and riding breeches and his black hair was neatly combed and still damp from his shower. She would never grow tired of looking at him, Sara thought.

"Keep looking at me like that, girl," he said softly, "and we won't have to tell him anything." Sara flushed a little and he reached out and traced the curve of her cheek, his fingers light and cool against her skin. "Come along with you, and we'll beard the lion in his den."

Aronsen looked up when they came out to the terrace together, and smiled genially. "Good morning," he said impartially to the two of them. "Sit down, sit down."

Sara made a gesture toward a chair, then glanced at Daniel. He hadn't moved. She stopped and he said to her grandfather without preamble, "I've come to give you my notice, sir."

The genial expression did not leave Aronsen's face. "Ah. You're going back to Ireland, then?"

"Yes." Daniel's face was expressionless. I bought two of Harold Price's mares to take back with me. I'm going to breed jumpers, sir—breed them and train them."

"Not much money in jumpers, Daniel," Aronsen said noncommittally. Sara stood midway between the two men and felt invisible.

"Not a fortune, no," Daniel replied. "But steeplechasing is a much bigger industry in Ireland and England than it is here. It's a living." He didn't look at Sara but extended his hand. She put hers into it and he said, still looking at her grandfather, "I have asked Sara to marry me, Mr. Aronsen, and she has agreed."

Sara was looking at Daniel's still, grave face and not at her grandfather. "She has, has she?" Aronsen said, and Sara glanced at him quickly. His smile, if anything, had broadened. "Sit down, sit down, the two of you, and let's discuss this for a little."

Daniel moved toward the table and Sara followed. He held a chair for her and then sat down himself, facing Aronsen. "I'm not so surprised, you see," her grandfather said to Sara. "Last night I told your mother I thought Daniel had beaten B.J. out."

Sara's eyes widened in surprise. "You did?"

Aronsen chuckled. "I see more than you give me credit for." He turned to Daniel. "So you plan to go back to Ireland, eh?"

"Yes, sir."

"When?"

"September. Sara and I thought we'd get married here before I go."

"I see, I see." Aronsen looked over the top of Sara's head and said, "Good morning, Lori. You've just walked in on an engagement announcement."

Lorraine was coming down the steps dressed in matching pale green slacks and shirt. With her small, perfect figure and feathery blond hair, she didn't look more than thirty, Sara thought. Then her mother's face hardened and a few age lines seemed to creep in.

"What!" she said, coming over to stand between her father and Sara.

Daniel had risen at her approach and now he said composedly, "Sara and I are going to be married, Mrs. Burnett."

"Married!" Lorraine stared at her daughter. "Is this true?"

"Yes, it is, Mother," Sara said, and looked not at Lorraine but at Daniel.

"Married to a farmworker!"

Not a muscle in Daniel's face moved. "Not a farmworker, Mother, a farm owner," Sara said firmly. "Daniel has his own farm in Ireland."

Lorraine snorted and looked at Daniel. "What kind of a farm?" she asked skeptically.

"A horse farm, Mrs. Burnett. Near Bansha in County Tipperary."

"A horse farm." Lorraine sat down and Daniel slowly followed suit, watching her all the time, his blue eyes steady and inscrutable. "I'll bet it's nothing like Canfield," Lorraine said ironically.

"It's nothing so grand as Canfield," Daniel replied pleasantly, "but it's mine."

"Lorraine opened her mouth again, but her father cut in. "Well, now, if you will excuse us, ladies, Daniel and I have business matters to discuss—like the question of his successor. Come along into the office with me, son, and we'll leave the women to have their breakfast."

"Yes, sir," said Daniel, and bestowed a small, encouraging smile on Sara before he followed her grandfather into the house.

Chapter 12

"Are you insane?" Lorraine asked her daughter.

"No. I love him, Mother. I'm going to marry him."

"Oh—love," Lorraine said cynically. "And do you think love is going to see you through life on some Irish pig farm?"

"It's *not a* pig farm," Sara said angrily. "I won't let you talk that way, Mother."

"All right," Lorraine replied in a milder voice, "so it's not a pig farm. But it's not the life you were raised for, darling. Oh, I know you don't think money is important; it never is when you've always had it. But try doing without it and you'll soon learn how important it is."

"I don't care," Sara said. "All I care about is Daniel."

Lorraine's lips thinned. "I know," she said. "He's gotten you into bed with him and now you think he can walk on water. Well, sex isn't enough to hold a marriage together, Sara. And believe me, you're talking to someone who knows."

Sara's cheeks were very flushed. "It isn't just sex, Mother, it's *love.*"

"Oh God," said Lorraine, "the young. So it's love. But will you tell me, darling, how you are going to cope as a farmer's wife? He's going to expect you to cook and clean and do his laundry and help muck out his manure. He's probably Catholic and you'll end up having a new baby every year. No theaters, no restaurants, none of the cultural things you've taken for granted all your life. God, he probably doesn't read anything but horse magazines."

Sara bit her lip. "Daniel went to school with the Jesuits in Ireland, Mother. He's had a better education than I have! And as for the rest of it, I'm sure I can do it. Other girls manage, so why can't I?"

"Because you weren't brought up as a peasant," Lorraine said shortly.

Sara stood up. "I really don't care to continue this conversation, Mother," she said coldly, and went into the house and up to her room.

But her mother's words had fallen on fertile ground. It was not the description of a life without cultural amenities that disturbed Sara; it was her own sense of inadequacy. She was afraid she would not be able to pull her weight. And recently she had begun to be afraid of something else.

She was late with her period and that was unusual for her. What was more, the last few mornings she had awoken feeling distinctly queasy. Sara was beginning to be afraid she was pregnant.

It would not be at all surprising, she thought now as she sat on her window seat staring blindly out across the rolling acres of pasture. Neither she nor Daniel had taken any precautions over the past few weeks.

With a baby her life in Ireland was certainly not going to be Love's Young Dream, as her mother would so scornfully say. A baby was no dream. A baby was a very grave responsibility. She would love Daniel's baby, there was no question about that. But would she be able to take care of it? And she would be in strange and probably primitive surroundings, with no one she knew nearby.

Her stomach heaved a little and Sara closed her eyes. It was more likely a stomach virus, she thought. In a day or two she would feel better.

*

After dinner that evening Sara said to her mother and grandfather, "I'm going down to see Daniel for a while." There was a trace of defiance in her voice. Her grandfather smiled; her mother looked cynical but didn't object. Sara took her car and parked it squarely in front of Daniel's cottage.

The dogs set up their usual ruckus and Daniel came to the door. He had not been expecting her.

He looked terrible: he was bare to the waist and filthy. "Sara," he said on a note of surprise. "Come in, girl."

Sara laughed. Just seeing him lifted her heart. "Whatever are you doing?" she asked.

He ran a dust-blackened hand through his hair. There was a line of dirt across one elegant cheekbone. "Trying to clear out all the junk I've thrown in the attic for the past three years." He shook his head in astonishment. "I don't seem to have ever thrown anything out." He looked at her crisp pink dress. "Can you stay?"

"Yes. I told Mother and Grandpa I was coming down to see you."

He nodded, then smiled faintly. "Why don't you sit down, and I'll go and shower."

"A very good idea," Sara said.

He showered and Sara looked through the books on the small bookcase under the window. There was a TV in the room, but it had broken a year ago and Daniel had never bothered to get it repaired. He had rarely watched it anyway, he told Sara, preferring to listen to the news on the radio.

Sara was turning the pages of a paperback edition of *The Mediterranean in the Age of Philip II* when Daniel came back into the living room. She looked over her shoulder at him. He had put on a clean pair of jeans, but was still barefoot and shirtless. "This book looks terribly deep," Sara said.

He came up behind her and looked at the title. "I like history," he said, and took the book from her unresisting hand. "But I like you better." And he bent his head and began to kiss her. They progressed from the living room to the bedroom rather rapidly.

This was what she had come for, Sara thought drowsily as she lay next to Daniel and listened to the slow sound of his breathing. This was home, here in his arms. It didn't matter where she lived, this would always be home. And it wasn't just the physical excitement of sex, as her mother thought. It was the sweetness of his love. She could feel it always—his tenderness, his sureness, his quality of always being there with her.

The curtains at the window began to blow and they could hear the sound of rain against the roof. Daniel got out of bed.

"I'd better close the windows," he said, and made a tour of the house. Sara listened for the sound of his footsteps. They were hard to hear, he walked so lightly.

"You would have made a good guerrilla," she said as he got back into bed with her. "The enemy would never be able to hear you coming—you walk like a cat."

"The Irish fought a guerrilla war for seven hundred years. I suppose it got into the bloodlines." He was lying with his hands crossed behind his head and she looked lovingly at his profile in the dimness of the room. "Will you mind going to see Father Baines at Holy Trinity?" he asked.

Sara replied doubtfully, "I'm afraid I don't know an awful lot about religion, Daniel. It wasn't exactly Mother's strong suit."

"Do you tell me? But you needn't worry about Father Baines, girl. He won't put you through the catechism. There's no need for you to turn Catholic, you know." He paused then added. "He will want you to promise to bring our children up Catholic, though."

"Well ... that would be all right with me."

At that he turned, pushing himself up on his elbow. "If you don't want a baby right away," he said soberly, "we should start to take some precautions."

The temptation to tell him that it might be a little late for precautions was very strong. She hesitated, then said, "Would you want a baby right away?"

"It makes no difference to me," he answered, "but I think it would be hard on you, love. We'd do better to wait."

"Yes," said Sara a little hollowly. "It probably would be better." At that he reached out with his arm, rolling so that he lay close beside her, his arm around her waist, his head on her breast. She looked down at his dark head. "I wish I didn't have to leave." Outside, the rain had turned to a steady downpour.

"Soon," he murmured, his mouth against her skin, "soon you won't have to leave at all. It will be just we two together."

Sara stroked his thick black hair. "Mrs. Daniel Riordan," she whispered. "It sounds just lovely."

"The seven Kings of Tara were not richer than I am." He kissed the hollow between her breasts.

"Daniel," she whispered. His warm, seeking mouth moved along the full white curve and then touched the nipple. Sara's hand in his hair tensed.

"You have skin like flowers." His mouth moved to her other breast. Sara's breathing grew ragged. "Skin like flowers and a mouth like honey." He was poised over her now, supporting himself on his hands. She arched up toward him. Their mouths were very close. "Sara," he said, "love of my soul." And then they were together.

*

Two days after Sara's visit to Father Baines, William Aronsen offered Daniel Canfield Farm. He called Daniel and Sara into his office in the afternoon and with obvious pleasure made his proposition.

"I have no son, Daniel, and my daughter has no interest in this farm. There will be plenty of money for Lori, but I want the farm to go to someone who will love it. Sara loves it. And she's marrying a boy who has horses in his blood." Sara stared at her grandfather incredulously as he went on. "I want you to give up this scheme of going to Ireland, Daniel. I want you to stay here and take on the job of managing the entire farm. When I die, I'll leave it all to you and Sara."

Sara's heart leapt. To stay here! How wonderful!

"Oh, Grandpa," she said in a quivering voice. She felt tears coming to her eyes. *"Thank* you." Aronsen smiled at her. Then they both turned to Daniel.

He was very pale under his tan. "Well, son," Aronsen asked, "what do you say?"

"Thank you very much, sir," Daniel said in a low, steady voice. "You are very generous. But I cannot accept your offer."

Aronsen's thunderstruck "What?" clashed with Sara's cry of "Daniel!"

"I am sorry. It's a grand offer you're making me, but I must go back to Ireland."

Sara's hands clenched in her lap and she stared at her fiancé's set face. There were lines bracketing his mouth. The perfectly straight nose looked thinner somehow, the cheekbones more prominent. He looked at her. "When I asked you to marry me, I told you I was a poor man," he said. "I'll be taking no handouts from your family."

"God Almighty, boy!" Aronsen almost shouted. "This isn't a handout! I'm offering you a place here as my grandson."

No feature of Daniel's face moved, but Sara could see the muscles tense beneath the deeply tanned skin. "I know that," he said. "And I thank you, sir. But I cannot accept."

Aronsen turned to his granddaughter. "What do you say, Sara?"

Sara's face was troubled. "Are you sure, Daniel?" she asked softly.

His eyes met hers. "Yes."

"It's pride, that's what it is," Aronsen snapped. "Goddamn stupid pride."

"Yes," said Daniel again. "It is."

The two men looked at each other.

"You can't eat pride," Sara's grandfather said.

"We will not have to. The farm will support us fine."

There was silence as the two men continued to look at each other. "You're a stubborn Irish bastard," Aronsen said then. Daniel said nothing. "Pride was Lucifer's downfall," the older man added.

Daniel's face closed. He rose. "Thank you for your offer, sir. I'm sorry to have disappointed you. Will that be all now?"

"Yes, dammit."

Daniel walked toward the door and Sara half-rose from her chair to follow. "Stay a moment, Sara. I want to talk to you," Aronsen said. Then, as Sara still hesitated, Daniel turned to her.

"Stay, girl. I'll be at the yearling barn if you want me."

He was gone and Sara subsided into her chair and turned to face her grandfather.

*

It was almost an hour later when finally she sought out Daniel. He was playing with Fergus behind the barn, trying to pull a stick from the dog's mouth while the dog tried to hang onto it. He stopped when he saw her.

"Grandpa is upset," Sara said.

"I'm sorry for that."

Fergus tried to get Daniel to play some more. Daniel shook his head at the dog and said, "No, Fergus. No more. Go find Deirdre." He turned to Sara. "Let's walk." Then, as they began to move toward the paddock area, "Have I upset you?"

"A little," Sara replied. "It just seems such a perfect opportunity, Daniel. Everything you've ever worked for falling so neatly into your lap. It doesn't make sense to turn it down."

"The only work I've ever done to earn Canfield Farm," Daniel said harshly, "is in bed." Then, as Sara recoiled a little in hurt shock, "I'm sorry, girl, but it's true, and you know it. And I will not be" having it said that Daniel Riordan is a fortune hunter—a creature like one of those bloodsuckers your mother is always marrying."

Now Sara was angry. "I never thought you cared a damn about what other people thought of you! You're a humbug, Daniel Riordan. I know the truth about you, and so do you. But because of stupid pride, you're turning down the greatest thoroughbred racing farm in America."

Daniel's face was bleak. "I cannot help it, that's how I am."

Sara looked up at his profile and tried another tack. "Grandpa's a lonely old man, Daniel. Can't you see that?"

He stopped. "Yes, I can see that. And I can see where I fit very nicely into his dynastic plans. But I have plans of my own, Sara, and they are all centered in Ireland. I'm an Irishman. I like Americans—I like America. But I'm an Irishman and I want to go home. If you want to come with me, fine. But Ireland's where I am going. If you want Canfield, you'll have to have it without me."

He meant it. He meant every word. Nothing she could say or do would ever change his mind.

"If you want to back out of our engagement," he said coldly, "I shall understand perfectly."

"No." Sara shook her head. "Of course I don't want to back out, Daniel. How can you say that?" She stepped closer to him and then she was in his arms. They held each other tightly for a long minute; then he kissed her hair and put her away.

"I don't know," he said a little wearily. "Perhaps I'm not being fair to you—taking your heritage away from you like this."

Now that she had stopped fighting him, his conscience was beginning to stir, she thought. "I'd rather have you," she said.

"I *cannot* accept Canfield, Sara."

She put her cheek against his shoulder. "Yes. All right, Daniel. I understand."

She wouldn't change him. She told her grandfather about their conversation. "He said he wasn't like one of the creatures Mother is always marrying, Grandpa. He isn't going to change his mind, you know. I don't think Daniel ever changes his mind."

Reluctantly Aronsen came to the same conclusion and gave up trying to persuade Daniel to stay. "You're an even tougher bird than I am, Daniel," he said to his future grandson, and managed to present Daniel with a stallion for a wedding present.

Daniel was thrilled with the stallion, and Sara tried to be thrilled too, but these days her mind was preoccupied with one thing only. The morning queasiness had gotten worse, not better, and she was still late with her period.

Once or twice she caught Daniel looking at her with an odd expression in his eyes. She thought perhaps he was afraid she was regretting their engagement. He asked her once if she wanted to postpone their wedding for a few months and she said no.

She was just afraid of everything. She found herself crying for no apparent reason. She scolded herself for being a baby, but she couldn't seem to help herself.

Finally she decided to go into Lexington to a clinic she found in the Yellow Pages and have a pregnancy test.

Chapter 13

The people in the clinic were brisk and efficient and didn't seem to notice her lack of a wedding ring. They told her they would call her in twenty-four to forty-eight hours. Sara was feeling quite tense when she left the clinic and decided to do a little shopping to distract herself. Just outside a department store she ran into B.J. Debrett. On the spur of the moment she stopped and had lunch with him. Then, when he escorted her back to her car, they found it wouldn't start again. B.J. said he'd run her home. They were on the main road leading out of Lexington toward Canfield when a car ran a light and cut in front of them.

"Stupid son of a bitch," B.J. muttered. He looked at Sara. "Are you all right?"

"Yes." B.J. had slammed on the brake but Sara's seat belt had held her firmly. "What an idiot," she said.

B.J. grunted. The car was racing ahead of them down the road. The light changed from green to red but the car didn't stop.

"The bastard's going to run another light," B.J. said.

What happened next was to replay itself over and over in Sara's nightmares. At the change of light, a man on a motorcycle moved from the street on their right into the intersection. The car in front of them, running through the red light, smashed right into the motorcycle, sending it flying into the air. A woman screamed. The car in front of them came to a halt. B.J. swore.

Sara was out of the car and running. There was already a group of people around the man on the pavement. Sara threw herself down next to the limp, unconscious figure.

"Daniel," she cried in anguish. *"Daniel!"*

"Do you know him, Miss?" asked a male voice.

"Oh my God." It was B.J. He knelt down in the street next to her and put his head on Daniel's chest.

"He's alive." He looked up. "Has anyone called for an ambulance?"

"My friend went to call," someone said.

"Don't move him," B.J. said. He stood up, pulling Sara with him. "Hang on, Sara," he said. "Help is on the way." He put his arm tightly around her.

There was the click of a camera and Sara looked up to find a photographer taking her picture as she huddled next to B.J.

A siren sounded down the street. Sara pulled away from B.J. and dropped down once again next to Daniel. She was afraid to touch him, afraid she would hurt him even more. There was blood all over the leg of his jeans. She was completely unaware of the tears that were streaming down her face.

It seemed an eternity before they got him into the ambulance. His eyes opened once when they moved him, looking at Sara without recognition. Then they closed again. Sara and B.J. got into the ambulance, and as they pulled away, Sara saw two policemen standing next to the car that had hit Daniel.

The attendants had taken off Daniel's helmet, and his head and face looked unscathed. He was deathly pale.

"I can't get a pulse," one of the attendants said to the other.

"What do you mean, you can't get a pulse?" Sara cried frantically. "He's breathing! I can see him breathing!"

"I can't get a pulse in his leg, Miss," the man said.

Next to Sara B.J. said in a low voice, "Jesus God."

They swept into the emergency entrance of the hospital, sirens wailing, where a doctor and two nurses were waiting for them. They wheeled Daniel away almost immediately. The attendant who had been with them on the ambulance stopped to talk to a nurse. B.J. heard him say, "He's going to lose a leg."

B.J. glanced quickly at Sara to see if she had heard. "He won't," she said. "I won't let that happen."

"Sit down for a minute, Sara," B.J. said helplessly. "I'm going to call your grandfather."

Aronsen and Lorraine had reached the hospital by the time the doctor, who knew William Aronsen, came back to report.

"He's pretty badly smashed up, Bill," Dr. Barr said bluntly. "The helmet seems to have saved his head, but he has a broken arm, a broken wrist, several broken ribs, and a broken left leg. The break isn't the biggest problem with the leg, though. Both the arteries are injured. He's got no blood supply to the lower part of the leg."

"Jesus," said William Aronsen.

Sara's face was stark but her voice was steady. "There must be something you can do."

"I have a call in to our vascular surgeon. But the boy's in deep shock."

"What can the vascular surgeon do?" asked Sara.

"An arterial graft. Maybe.'

"When will he be here?"

"He's on his way. I'll have him talk to you after he's seen Daniel."

"Thanks, Howard," replied Aronsen. Sara said nothing.

The vascular surgeon came in twenty-five minutes later. "I'm going to try an arterial graft," he said after he had introduced himself. "If I don't, he'll lose the leg."

Sara's face was still. "Then do it."

"Right, then," Dr. Morgenstern said briskly. "We'll get him ready to go."

"I want to see him," said Sara.

There was a pause, then Dr. Morgenstern said, "All right, but just for a minute. He's in our intensive-care unit. It's this way."

Daniel was hooked up to an I.V. He was unconscious, and white as the sheets he was lying on.

Sara gripped the iron edge of his bed so tightly that her knuckles showed white. The ground felt shaky under her feet. I will not faint, she thought fiercely. *I will not faint.*

"Sara." It was her grandfather's hand under her arm. "Dr. Barr says there's a room we can wait in. Come along now."

Two nurses went over to Daniel. A man dressed in black came into the room, and turning, Sara saw that it was Father Baines. He gave her an encouraging smile and went over to Daniel's side. Sara saw that he had a small black bag with him.

Sara turned and allowed her grandfather to take her out of the room.

Dr. Barr showed them to a room with several armchairs and a sofa, all in the Danish modern style. The upholstery was royal blue. The floor was white, no-wax linoleum. Sara sat down in one of the chairs, clasped her hands together, and stared straight ahead.

"He's in shock," she said. "He could die under the anesthetic."

"Daniel's a tough customer, Sara." It was B.J.'s voice coming to her as if from a great distance. "He'll make it all right."

Sara didn't answer.

"You don't have to wait, B.J.," Aronsen said.

"Of course I'll wait. I just want to call my grandparents and tell them what's happened. I think I saw a phone down the hall."

B.J. made his call and then came back. Lorraine sat with them on the sofa and said nothing. Aronsen paced the room.

Father Baines came in. "Sara?" His voice was deep, rumbly, and kind. "I just thought I'd look in to see how you were doing."

Sara had risen when she saw the priest in the doorway. She went over to him now and he took her hand in a comforting clasp. "He's a strong young man. And Dr. Morgenstern is excellent. Remember that."

Sara stared at him out of huge golden eyes. "Did you give Daniel the Last Rites?"

"We don't call it Last Rites anymore," he said reassuringly. "It's the Sacrament of the Sick. And it doesn't mean Daniel is going to die. Quite the opposite, in fact. It is often very strengthening."

Sara swallowed hard.

"Pray, Sara," the priest said gently. "And I will pray also."

"Thank you, Father," Sara whispered. Then she turned to introduce him to the others in the room.

After Father Baines had gone, Sara went back to sitting in the blue chair.

"God," Lorraine said, in almost the first words she had spoken all afternoon, "this reminds me of the times I waited in the hospital for Johnny."

Sara turned to look at Lorraine and for a brief moment mother and daughter were closer than they had been in twenty-four years.

Two hours went by. B.J. went out for coffee, which he and Aronsen and Lorraine drank. Sara's lay untouched.

Three hours went by. When Aronsen went to the desk to inquire, he was told that Daniel was still in the operating room.

"There's a coffee shop downstairs," he said to them when he came back. "Let's go and get something to eat."

"I'm not hungry," Sara said automatically.

"You need something, darling," her mother said briskly. "Come along. We'll only be downstairs."

Reluctantly Sara went with the others to the coffee shop, but she could not eat the turkey club sandwich her mother ordered for her.

"I have to get back upstairs," she told her grandfather.

"Honey, there's nothing you can do. He's still in the operating room."

"I know that, Grandpa. I just have to *be* there."

"All right." B.J. stood up next to her. "You finish your sandwiches. I'll go back with Sara."

Five hours went by.

Daniel! Oh, Daniel! Save him for me, God, Sara prayed. Save him for me and I'll do anything. I'll be so strong, so good...

Daniel, my love.

Seven hours went by. Sara was sitting in the same blue chair when the door opened and Dr. Morgenstern still in operating-theater garb, came in. He looked exhausted.

Sara jumped to her feet.

"The surgery was successful," he said to her. "The graft is working."

Sara's knees went weak. "How ... how is he?"

"He's back in the intensive-care unit. He did well. He should be okay—if the graft continues to hold up."

"*Thank you*, Doctor." Sara tried to smile but the doctor's face was blurring.

"Grab her," Dr. Morgenstern said sharply, and B.J. did just that as Sara began to slide neatly to the ground.

*

Sara's grandfather and her mother drove her home. She insisted on stopping at Daniel's cottage to pick up the dogs.

"We can't just leave them alone in the house," she said to her mother's protest.

"Surely one of the men can look after them."

"No. They're Daniel's dogs and they know me. I'm going to bring them home."

It was early morning when they finally reached Canfield Farm, and Sara was exhausted. Yet as soon as she closed her eyes, she would see that car flying through the intersection and smashing into Daniel's motorcycle. It was after four when she finally fell asleep.

She awoke at nine o'clock and was sick in the bathroom. She dressed and went downstairs, feeling nausea sweep over her again as she reached the dining room. She sat down, rigid and upright, and waited for it to pass. She *would* not be sick again.

"Are you all right, Miss Sara?" Benjy, who worked in her grandfather's kitchen, asked.

"Yes," she replied through clenched teeth. "I'm fine, Benjy. Is Grandpa up yet?"

"Not yet, Miss Sara."

"Tell him when he gets up that I've gone to the hospital."

"Don't you want breakfast, miss?"

Sara closed her eyes briefly. "No." She stood up and remembered something. "My car. My car wouldn't start yesterday. Is it still in Lexington?"

"I reckon it is, Miss Sara. It ain't out here as far as I know."

"I'll take Grandpa's car, then," Sara said ruthlessly. "Will you tell him that too, Benjy?"

"Yes, miss. I'll tell him."

Sara drove her grandfather's Cadillac to the hospital, fighting nausea the whole way. At the front desk they told her Daniel was still in the intensive-care unit.

Sara's heart lurched when she first saw him. He was covered with casts and bandages and seemed to be surrounded by I.V. tubes. But his eyelashes lifted when she came to stand beside him and the heavy blue eyes recognized her.

"How are you feeling, darling?" she asked, her lips pale.

"Alive. I suppose that's something." His voice was low and slightly slurred. His eyes looked almost black. Sara supposed he must be heavily sedated.

"You were in the operating room for seven hours," she told him, and saw his eyes widen in surprise. "But you're going to be fine, Daniel. Everything will mend."

His lids began to close. "You okay?" he asked.

"Yes. I'm fine." She looked around for a chair she could pull up to the bed.

His eyes opened again. "Don't go," he said strongly.

"I'm not going," she replied. "I'm going to stay right here. I only want to get a chair."

He seemed satisfied by her reply; his eyes closed again. Sara pulled a chair up beside him and sat down.

Chapter 14

Sara was still sitting there when B.J. and her grandfather came in three hours later.

"How is he?" Aronsen asked gruffly.

"Sleeping mostly," Sara replied. "They have him pretty well doped up."

B.J. looked at Daniel's face on the pillow. Haggard, unshaved, drugged into exhausted sleep, it was still beautiful. He looked from Daniel to Sara. "You look exhausted," he said to her, and his voice came out rougher than he had intended.

She summoned up the ghost of a smile. "I'm all right. Grandpa, perhaps you can find Dr. Morgenstern and get a report. He hasn't been by here since I arrived."

"I'll try," Aronsen said, and walked out of the room.

"It was nice of you to come, B.J.," Sara said.

"I drove your grandfather. It seems you absconded with his car."

"Um." Sara's eyes were on Daniel's face and her voice sounded distracted. She seemed to be scarcely aware of B.J.'s presence. "I guess I did." She didn't say anything else until Aronsen returned with Dr. Morgenstern in tow.

*

Sara spent the following two weeks sitting by Daniel's side. The arterial graft held up and the other artery in the back of his leg mended itself and began to function. Ten days after the first operation, they took Daniel back to the operating room to close up a hole that had been torn in his left calf. That operation took five hours; it too was successful.

Sara hardly left the hospital. Through all the anguish, fear, and exhaustion, one thing only sustained her. Daniel needed her. He didn't say much, but she saw how his eyes followed her when she moved about his room. She saw the look on his face when she came in the door. He was weak and in pain and so frighteningly vulnerable. He needed her.

She seldom left his side. She thought of nothing, was aware of nothing, except this one room and this one man who was depending on her to be there for him. Her grandfather came and went; her mother came every day for the first week and then left for New York. B.J. was a constant visitor.

B.J. was the only one to know her secret. He had driven her home from the hospital on that first day and had come into the house for a minute. He was standing next to her when the telephone rang. Sara picked it up instantly.

"Hello?" she said in a strained voice. "Yes, this is she." Then, as B.J. watched with concern, warm color flushed into her cheeks.

"It was positive," she said. "You're sure? Yes. Thank you." She hung up the phone.

"What was that?" B.J. asked.

Sara looked at him, her eyes curiously blank. "That was the lab," she said. "I'm pregnant."

B.J. could feel the blood begin to thump in his neck below the ears. "I see." His heart was beating strangely and unsteadily. "Does Daniel know?"

"No." Sara's vision seemed to clear. "No! And he mustn't be told. Not now. I shouldn't have told you."

"Don't worry. I'll keep my mouth shut."

She gave him a shadowy smile. "That's where I was yesterday when I ran into you. At the lab." She put an unsteady hand on her forehead. "Oh, *Daniel.*" The way she said it caught B.J. by the throat.

"He'll be all right, Sara," he heard himself say. Somehow his arm had found its way around her shoulders. "You must try to take care of yourself, too. Go get some sleep. You're worn out."

"Yes." She put her hand over his where it lay on her shoulder and gave it a brief squeeze. "Thank you, B.J. You're such a good friend."

*

A good friend—that was how she saw him. When she saw him at all, that is. It often seemed to B.J. that no one was real to Sara except Daniel.

B.J. was in Daniel's room the afternoon William Aronsen spoke of his future grandson's coming home.

"You won't be on your feet for months, son," Aronsen said. "There's no way you and Sara are going to Ireland now. Come home to Canfield to recuperate first. Get back your strength—then we'll talk about Ireland."

Daniel's thin muscular hands moved slightly on the sheet. His face, however, was still.

"You're very kind, sir," he said after a minute.

Aronsen smiled. "Not at all. We're going to take good care of you, Daniel, make no mistake about that."

Daniel did not look at Sara, or at any of them. His eyes seemed to be focused on something on the far side of the room.

"Yes," he said, and there was the faintest undercurrent of repressed feeling in his voice. "Yes, I can see that you are."

Sara followed B.J. out of Daniel's room when he left.

"Can you stop for a cup of coffee, B.J.?" she asked. "I have to talk to you."

"Sure."

They went to the hospital coffee shop and sat facing each other across a small table.

"I want to take Daniel's horses to Ireland," she said bluntly. "Will you help me?"

"What!"

Sara's hair was fastened at the nape of her neck and the fluorescent lights of the coffee shop shone on the smooth, coppery crown of her head. Her tan had faded in the last weeks and her skin was the color of creamy magnolias. Her face looked thinner, her eyes larger.

"You saw what happened just now," she said. "Grandpa is going to take advantage of Daniel's weakness and drag him home to Canfield."

"Sara," B.J. said patiently, "your grandfather is right. Daniel is in no shape to run a farm right now."

"I know that. Daniel knows that. That's why he's so miserable. But Daniel's not going to run the farm. I am."

B.J. could feel his eyes widening. *"You?"*

Sara's smile was a little shadowy. "Me," she said.

"Sara, you can't possibly undertake something like that alone."

Sara stirred her coffee. "A few weeks ago, I would have agreed with you, B.J. A few weeks ago I was worried whether I could learn to cook and clean and keep house." She laughed. "Isn't it astonishing how trivial all our other worries seem when we're struck by real catastrophe?"

B.J. didn't say anything and she continued, looking abstractedly at her coffee cup, seeming almost to be talking to herself. "Grandpa offered Canfield to Daniel, did you know that?" She glanced up as B.J. shook his head in surprise. "Oh yes. A few weeks before the accident. And Daniel turned him down."

"That doesn't surprise me," B.J. said.

"No. It wouldn't surprise anyone who knew Daniel. He feels very strongly about it, B.J. He doesn't want Canfield, doesn't want people to think he's a fortune hunter. He wants to go home to Ireland." She drew a deep, slow breath. "I wanted him to stay in Kentucky, I must admit. But he wouldn't."

B.J. stirred some milk into his coffee. "And now he's going to have to."

"Now he's going to have to. He's trapped, don't you see? Trapped by his weakness, by his leg. He can't do anything for himself. And Grandpa will bring him home, and board his mares, and pay all his bills—and then Daniel will be even more trapped. The baby will just be the icing on the cake."

"I thought you said you wanted him to stay in Kentucky."

Sara shook her head. "Not like this, not against his will. It will eat him up, B.J. It will destroy him—it will destroy *us*. And so, since he can't do anything for himself, I have to do it for him." She smiled a little, her lovely full mouth curving tenderly. "Isn't it amazing how simple things become when you don't have any choice? I always had someone to lean on, someone to tell me what to do and how to do it. I never thought I could do anything for myself." She looked at him directly and said with devastating simplicity, "But now it's time for me to be strong. Now it's time for me to grow up."

B.J. rested his elbows on the table and linked his hands together. "Has Daniel asked you to go?"

She shook her head. "He hasn't said a word to me about any of this, B.J. But I know what he must be feeling."

"Do you plan to stay in Ireland, then?"

"Yes. I'll stay and wait for Daniel. He should be able to travel in six weeks or so."

B.J. pressed his lips against his clenched hands. There was a stubborn pain in his throat and he had a hard time speaking around it. "What if Daniel doesn't want you to go?"

"I'm going anyway. We can't begin our marriage under Grandpa's roof. It would be disastrous." She looked at him steadily. "Will you help me, B.J.? For Daniel's sake?"

For Daniel's sake. It was all for Daniel's sake. For Daniel's sake she would walk barefoot over hot coals—and she would walk over B.J., use him, and forget him as if he were an inanimate thing with no feelings of his own.

"All right," he said harshly. "All right, Sara. I'll help you."

She smiled at him. "Thank you, B.J. We're so lucky to have a friend like you."

*

"So it's all set," Sara said to Daniel. "The horses and I are flying out next Tuesday. I brought a notebook to fill up with your instructions."

Daniel stared at her incredulously. "You've taken leave of your senses, girl. You can't take the horses to Ireland by yourself."

"I can and I will." Sara smiled at him serenely. "You'll have to arrange for transport from the airport to the farm. I haven't the foggiest idea whom to call. And you'll have to tell me where to buy feed, and how much to give, and all that stuff."

"You can't do it," Daniel repeated. His too-thin face was slightly flushed.

Sara stared at him. "Why not?" she demanded. "Do I look like an imbecile?"

He shifted a little in the bed. "Of course you don't look like an imbecile. But you don't know enough about horses."

"Daniel, I have been your virtual shadow for months now. I have been following you around like a little sponge—soaking up all your words of wisdom. I can do quite a lot, you know. I can groom, I can clip and blanket and do wraps and bandages. I can certainly dish up hay and grain—you do have to tell me how much, though. I can turn horses out and catch them and bring them into the barn again. I know how to use a telephone, so I can easily call the blacksmith and the vet when I need them." She raised her brows and stared at him. "So where is the problem?"

"I don't know," said Daniel. He began to laugh, then stopped. "What will your grandfather say?"

"It's not his affair," Sara replied. "It's ours." She gave him a severe look. "I'm not proposing to train these animals, remember. I will only attend to their bodily needs. And I want no part of any stallion. Montrose doesn't come until you do."

Daniel's blue eyes were brilliant. "It will be a couple of months."

"Yes," said Sara. "You're going to have to give me some money."

"There's a fellow I've employed to look after the place—Tim Maloney. He can help you." Daniel's voice sounded a little breathless.

"Great. Oh—and one other thing. Father Baines is coming tomorrow to marry us."

Daniel stared at her. "He is?"

"Yes. Ireland, I understand, is a very straight-laced country. If I'm going to go and live in your house, I want to do it respectably."

Daniel was laughing, though he lacked the breath for it. "Is there anything else you have to tell me?"

"No. It's you that have things to tell me." Sara took out her notebook and pen. "Now, about the feed."

Daniel was still talking, and Sara was writing furiously when B.J. came in an hour later. B.J. looked at his friend in the bed.

Daniel's face was lightly flushed and his eyes were bright. He seemed oblivious of all his casts and bandages. "How would you like to be my best man?" he asked B.J.

"When?" B.J. was clearly startled.

"Tomorrow." Daniel looked at Sara. "What time did you say?"

"Ten in the morning." Sara smiled at B.J. and then turned back to Daniel. "What was the name of that man with the hay?"

"I'll spell it for you," said Daniel, and proceeded to do so.

*

Sara got the horses to Shannon airport, where she was met by Tim Maloney, a wiry man of about sixty, with a van. They drove east in a soft Irish rain through a countryside of green fields surrounded by thick hawthorn hedges, until they came to Rathmore Farm, Daniel's home. Tim put the horses in the barn and his sister, Molly, met Sara in the house with tea and biscuits. Over the tea table Molly industriously gathered as much information as was humanly possible about the new residents of Rathmore Farm.

The following day Sara sent Daniel a telegram: "ARRIVED SAFELY. ALL IS WELL. SARA."

Sara had been far more apprehensive about this venture than she had allowed anyone to guess. She had been petrified that she would not be able to cope with Daniel's expensive thoroughbreds, that something would happen to them and it would be her fault. Nor had she known what to expect from the farmhouse—she'd had nightmare visions of no plumbing and no electricity.

It had all proved easier than she had feared. The house was old but it did have plumbing and electricity. The kitchen was ancient but the stove worked. There was no central heating, but there was a big fireplace in the living room and an electric heater in the bedroom.

The barns were beautiful. It was easy to see where Daniel had put his money.

Sara worked harder than she ever had in her life. She was up at dawn to go down to the barn to feed the horses and she was on the go until she fell into bed early to lie listening to the news report on Radio Eirann. She often did not make it through the news but fell asleep during the economic reporter's soporific drone.

She painted the house from top to bottom and with the help of Tim Maloney's sister made curtains for the windows. She covered the ancient furniture with bright material and bought new linen and towels and a new bedspread for the old four-poster in the master bedroom.

She missed Daniel and longed for him to come, but her waiting had a sweetness to it, too. She couldn't help but feel satisfaction with the job she was doing. She was learning to measure her own abilities and was beginning to grow in her own esteem. She *could* do this job; she *could* be *a helpmate* to Daniel; their marriage would be a partnership after all.

She was lonely, but her love for Daniel was like a flower planted within her, growing and blossoming even as the child in her womb grew and blossomed. She might be tired, her back might ache and her hands might be callused, but Sara herself bloomed.

Daniel flew into Shannon on an Aer Lingus flight one morning in late October. Sara waited outside the passport-control section with the other people who were meeting friends or relatives coming from America. It seemed she had been waiting forever, that everyone else had already come through, when the door opened at last and there was Daniel. His black hair, grown longer than she remembered it, had fallen over his forehead. He held a cane in his left hand. He looked around, saw her, and a flame showed, sudden and blue, in the depths of his eyes.

Sara had covered the twenty feet between them and was in his arms before she even realized she had moved. His cane clattered to the floor and he was kissing her eyelids and her cheeks and her mouth and she was clinging to him, laughing and crying all at once. The porter who carried Daniel's luggage regarded them with interest.

"Oh Daniel, oh Daniel, oh Daniel," Sara repeated over and over.

"Sara." He put his hands on her shoulders and held her away from him. "Let me look at you."

Her golden eyes gazed into his.

"Where are you after wanting this baggage?" the porter asked prosaically and, startled, they both turned to look at him.

"Oh. I have a car outside." Sara bent and picked up Daniel's cane. "It's this way. How is your leg, darling? How was the flight?"

"The leg is coming along." Sara noticed that he leaned noticeably on the cane. "I have a physical-therapy program to follow. It's for building up the muscles."

"You haven't used them in months. Of course they must be weak." Sara slowed her steps to match his. "Did you get any sleep on the plane?"

"No." He stopped and turned to look at her, his black hair blowing in the wind. "I was too excited."

Sara's eyes sparkled. "I know. I didn't get much sleep either."

Daniel's mouth tightened with pain when he got into the car, and Sara saw that there was sweat on his forehead. The day was cool and damp, and she wore a bulky sweater that covered the top of her slacks. She had not been able to button the slacks for several weeks. She got in next to him and put her cheek briefly against his shoulder. He picked up her hand.

"God," he said simply, "but it's good to be home."

*

He insisted on going down to the paddocks to see the horses before he came into the house. Tim had a fire going in the living-room fireplace when he got there. Daniel looked around the cozy room, deep surprise on his face.

"What have you done?" he asked Sara. "The barn used to look cozier than this room."

Sara's face glowed. "Oh," she said airily, "I just painted and put up some curtains and covered the furniture."

He was still looking around the room. "It's a palace you've made," he said. Then he put out a hand. "Come here by me, girl."

She went over and curled up on the sofa next to him. "Do you want a cup of tea?"

"Not right now," and he put an arm around her waist. It was not as slim as it had been a few months before. Sara felt him go very still. She reached down, put her hand over his, and moved it to her stomach.

"I'm afraid I've been keeping a secret from you," she said softly. "As you see, I had good reason for wanting us to get married when we did."

He drew in a long breath, harsh-sounding as a ratchet. "Why did you not tell me?"

"I didn't want to worry you." She removed his hand from her stomach and bent her head to kiss the strong, slender fingers. "I'm fine, Daniel. I went to a doctor in Limmerick, and he says I look terrific."

"When is the baby due?" His voice was terse, hard with controlled feeling.

"In March." She looked into his face and smiled. "You work very quickly, darling." Then, when he did not smile back, "You aren't pleased?"

"It's not that. It's this *bloody leg*. I'm not fit for hard work yet, Sara, and you—"

She stopped his mouth with a long kiss. "I'm not doing hard work," she said softly. "I'm not doing the stalls or dropping the hay. Tim is doing all that. All you have to do is get stronger, and you will. You want to look around for more horses, and you can do that now. Then, when you're better, you can start the training. The breeding program won't begin until February, and you'll be much stronger by then."

"You make it all sound so simple."

"It *is* simple, Daniel." She put her cheek down on his shoulder and closed her eyes. "Oh, I'm so *glad* you're here."

After a minute his fingers came down to touch her hair, slipping through the long, silky strands. She peeked up at him then, giving him a mischievous urchin's smile. "Haven't I been clever?" she asked.

He grinned, the first smile she had seen since he got off the plane. "It's a devil you are, Sara Riordan," he said. "I can see I'm going to have my hands full keeping you in order."

"That you are, darling," she replied serenely. She kissed him again. "That you are."

Chapter 15

It was a cool, damp spring morning when Lorraine Burnett walked into the arrivals lounge of Shannon airport and looked around for her daughter.

"Mother! Over here!" Lorraine turned and saw a tall slim girl with a baby balanced on her hip coming toward her. Sara wore tan corduroy pants and a maroon quilted vest. Her bright hair was cut short and her young face glowed with health and happiness. She gave her mother a kiss on the cheek and smiled. "How nice to see you."

"It's lovely to see you too, darling." Lorraine regarded her year-old black-haired, blue-eyed grandson with amazement. "How big Matthew has got."

Sara shifted her son to the other hip. "Big—and heavy. Where is your bag, Mother?"

Lorraine beckoned to a porter and then followed Sara out to an old blue Ford Anglia in the parking lot.

"This car is really rather ramshackle, darling," Lorraine said a little apprehensively as they drove out of the airport.

"I know," Sara replied cheerfully. "But it keeps on running—no thanks to Daniel, I might add. He's a genius with horses, but anything mechanical utterly bewilders him."

Sara shot confidently into the flow of traffic and they drove smoothly along the left-hand side of the street. "You've got used to driving the wrong way, I see," Lorraine remarked.

"Well," said Sara reasonably, "it's not the wrong way in Ireland."

"I suppose not." There was a pause. "How *is* Daniel?" Lorraine asked.

"He's fine. That thoroughbred mare he picked up in Kentucky is going great. Daniel's run her in some of the top English races and she's won or come second every time."

"That's wonderful," Lorraine said automatically.

"Yes. And Montrose had had quite a number of bookings. So things are looking very good for Rathmore Farm and the Riordans."

"If things are going so well, surely you could afford a better car," Lorraine murmured dryly.

"Ah," said Sara, "now that is a sore point with my husband. He'll spend the earth on a horse but it just about kills him to put money out on a machine." Sara expertly shifted gears. "And I rather like the old wreck. It's got character."

The Anglia hit a bump and Lorraine's teeth rattled. "It has lousy shocks, is what it has," she said acidly, and Sara laughed.

"You've cut your hair, darling," Lorraine said, gracefully changing the subject. "It's very becoming."

"Thanks. Daniel had a fit when I cut it off, but the Irish climate is so damp. It just never dried. I like it this way myself."

"Is Daniel at home?"

"Oh yes. He was slaving somewhere on the farm when I left." They were going through a small village and Sara opened the car window and called out, "How are you, Mr. Rafferty?"

The old man she had addressed turned to look at the car and his seamed face split into a huge smile. "It's yourself, Mrs. Riordan. And how is young Matthew these days?"

"Just fine, thank you," Sara called back. She waved and drove on as young Matthew woke up in the backseat and began to cry. "There's a bottle in that bag at your feet, Mother," Sara said. "Will you hand it to Matthew, please?" Lorraine did as requested, and silence descended over the backseat.

The sun broke out from behind the clouds as the Anglia pulled into the road that led to Rathmore Farm. Lorraine looked around the neatly fenced-in fields and then at the newly whitewashed farmhouse. Without speaking, she got out of the car. Sara leaned into the backseat to take Matthew out.

"Come in, Mother. It's almost time for lunch. Daniel should be in soon."

They went into the large, old-fashioned kitchen and Sara put the baby in a highchair. A delicious smell emanated from a pot on the stove.

"I've put you in the same bedroom you had last time you were here," Sara told her mother. "Why don't you go and get freshened up and then come on back down?"

"All right," said Lorraine, and slowly climbed the narrow wooden stairs to the small bedroom at the back of the second floor of the house. It was such a little house, Lorraine thought, and so antiquated. She didn't know how Sara could survive. She appeared to be doing more than just surviving, however. She appeared to be positively thriving.

Lorraine washed her hands in the ancient bathroom that serviced the entire family, adjusted her makeup before a tarnished mirror in the guestroom, and went back downstairs.

Sara was feeding Matthew his lunch. Lorraine sat down at the large round kitchen table and smiled at her grandson's intent face. The kitchen door banged open and two dogs trotted in, accompanied by their master.

"Hi, darling," Sara said. "Look who's here."

"How nice to see you, Lorraine," her son-in-law said. "I'm glad you decided to stop over at Shannon."

For an instant Lorraine didn't reply. It was always a shock, she thought, to encounter such absolute physical beauty in this shabby young Irishman wearing faded jeans and scarred leather riding boots. The dogs were circling around the kitchen, muddying up the floor, and Daniel put a hand on his wife's head.

"How did the car go?"

"Fine. I think Sean has done the trick. It didn't stall out once."

"Praise be."

"Lunch is ready, Daniel, if you want to wash up."

Daniel went up the stairs to the bathroom. The dogs stayed in the kitchen. Sara gave Matthew a cracker and went over to the stove.

Lunch was some kind of stew, and absolutely delicious.

"It's a chef I married," Daniel said when Lorraine complimented Sara. "I dine better than King Conchobar in Emain Macha." Matthew began to pound his fists on his high-chair tray, and Daniel laughed. "Matthew agrees."

"Why don't you take Matthew for a little walk while I clean up this kitchen?" Sara suggested. "Then it will be time for his nap."

"Come along, boyo," Daniel said, and scooping his son out of his chair, raised him to his shoulders. The baby shrieked with delight and held on to a large chunk of his father's thick black hair.

"Ouch." Daniel removed the small determined hands and wrapped the little fingers around his own. Sara opened the door as they exited into the sunshine along with the dogs.

Lorraine stood at the window watching Daniel walk down the gently sloping hill toward the barns. There was just the slightest of hesitations in his gait.

"The limp is almost completely gone," Lorraine said to Sara. "A year ago, when Matthew was born, it was still quite noticeable."

"Yes. It's about as good as it's going to get now. It still aches sometimes, and it isn't as strong as it once was, but he does very well. It hasn't interfered with his riding, thank God."

Lorraine came back to sit at the kitchen table. Sara was running water in the sink and expertly stacking the dishes.

"You work so hard, darling," Lorraine said.

"I suppose," Sara returned. She was remembering Daniel's gentle touch on her head; not a single strand of her shining hair had been disturbed. "We both do. But we like it."

"I guess you must." Lorraine was clearly bewildered. "You both certainly look marvelous."

Sara grinned. "It's the healthy outdoor life, Mother. And the Irish climate is so good for the skin."

Lorraine gazed at her daughter with wide, disingenuous eyes. "I'm going to get married again, Sara."

Oh Lord, Sara thought. She turned to her mother with a mixture of amusement and resignation. "Well, Mother, and who is the lucky guy this time?"

*

"Mother is getting married again," Sara told Daniel as they were undressing for bed that night.

He had taken off his shirt and the night-table lamp shone on the smoothly muscled brown flesh of his shoulders and chest. He gave her a look she couldn't quite read. "Ah, she's a fine adventuress, that mother of yours. And how many is this now?"

"Five," said Sara.

Daniel came over to sit on the side of the bed and bent to take off his boots. Sara, who was already in her nightgown and under the covers, reached out to put a hand on his bare back.

"Five," she repeated. "And none of them has lasted."

Daniel tossed his boots into the corner and straightened up. He turned to look at his wife. "Did she come just to tell you the good news?"

"I think so." Sara's hand slid around his back and came to rest on his bicep. "Poor Mother. I think she knows she's missed something very important in life, but she doesn't quite know what it is. Or maybe she does know—because she had it very briefly with my father—but she's afraid to admit it."

"And what would that be?" he asked, his voice low, his eyes intent upon her face.

"What we have," Sara answered. "Love."

His face did not alter. "I was under the impression that your mother thinks you are living in a slum. She kept looking around the kitchen tonight as if she thought it was going to fall down around her."

"That's nothing. You should have seen the way she looked at our car." Then, when he still didn't smile, "Daniel, surely you don't care what Mother thinks?"

"I don't know," he said slowly. "Tonight, all of a sudden, I looked at things through her eyes and..." He broke off and looked away from Sara to glance about the bedroom with its old, scarred furniture and worn rug. "What, after all, can I give you compared to what you've left?"

"Oh, nothing, nothing at all," Sara replied sarcastically. "Only yourself, whom I happen to love more than anything else on earth, and my son, and a home where I'm happy and busy and valued. What's all that, after all, when you compare it to Mother's eighteenth-century furniture and authentic Persian rugs?"

"Ah." His gaze returned to her face but now his eyes held a light that she recognized. "Of course, when you put it that way ..."

"I do put it that way. In point of fact, I put it that way emphatically."

"Emphatically, is it?" He leaned over her, his hands braced on either side of her shoulders, his face only a few inches away from hers.

"Emphatically," she repeated softly. Her eyelids felt heavy and a sweet, sensuous languor was creeping through her body. Her breathing deepened. His eyes were the dark blue they always turned when...

"*How* emphatically?" he asked gently.

His mouth was almost on hers. "Try me," she murmured, "and see." He slid the blanket down and ran a caressing hand all down the length of her breast, waist, hip, and thigh. They kissed deeply. "Of course," Sara said when his mouth finally left hers to travel down toward her throat and breast, "it's the wrong time of the month for Father Walsh's recommended rhythm method."

Daniel groaned and buried his face between her breasts. Sara smiled up at the ceiling and trailed her fingers through his hair. "On the other hand, I think Matthew would very much appreciate a little brother or sister."

Daniel didn't move. "Are you really meaning that?"

"Yes. I always hated being an only child."

"Matthew's only a year."

"They'll be good companions for each other, then."

"Ah, love," said Daniel. He raised his head and looked down at her, his lips curved in the quiet, intimate smile that only Sara had ever seen.

"I know. You're a lucky man, Daniel Riordan," Sara said.

The smile deepened. "I am that."

That smile of Daniel's just about dissolved her. He could smile like that at her in the middle of Shannon airport, she thought, and she would lie right down for him on the luggage carousel. She pictured the scene in her mind and chuckled.

"What's so funny?"

She shook her head, aching now, wanting him. His hands came down on her and her body ignited, flaming up for him in a sweet and heady bonfire of passion and surrender and love.

Afterward they lay close together, wrapped in comfort and peace. It was a long time before Daniel spoke.

"Persian rugs," he said, and laughed.

"Mmm. This is definitely better." Sara sounded sleepy.

"One day I'll give you Persian rugs," he said. "And fine rings for your fingers and golden chains for your lovely neck."

"A baby would be even nicer." Her head was pillowed on his shoulder and she turned her cheek to touch the bare skin of his chest with her lips.

"Ah well," he replied, "I'm trying, girl, I'm trying."

"Mmm. And very impressively, I must say." Her eyelids felt so heavy.

"Are you falling asleep on me?"

"No."

There was a two-minute silence. Sara had fallen asleep on his shoulder. "Ah well," said Daniel philosophically to the ceiling, "there's always tomorrow." And he reached out and turned off the bedroom light.

About the Author

Joan Wolf is a *USA TODAY* bestselling author whose highly reviewed books include some forty novels set in the period of the English Regency, earning her national recognition as a master of the genre. She fell in love with the Regency period when she was a young girl and discovered the novels of Georgette Heyer. Although she has strayed from the period now and then, it has always remained her favorite.

Joan was born and brought up in New York City, but has spent most of her adult life with her husband and two children in Connecticut. She has a passion for animals and over the years has filled the house with a variety of much-loved dogs and cats. Her great love for her horses has spilled over into every book she has written. The total number of her published novels is fifty-three, and she has no plans to retire.

"Joan Wolf never fails to deliver the best."
—Nora Roberts

"Joan Wolf is absolutely wonderful. I've loved her work for years."
—Iris Johansen

"As a writer, she's an absolute treasure."
—Linda Howard

"Strong, compelling fiction."
—Amanda Quick

"Joan Wolf writes with an absolute emotional mastery that goes straight to the heart."
—Mary Jo Putney

"Wolf's Regency historicals are as delicious and addictive as dark, rich, Belgian chocolates."
—Publishers Weekly

"Joan Wolf is back in the Regency saddle—hallelujah!"
—Catherine Coulter

* * *

To sign up for Joan's newsletter, email her at joanemwolf@gmail.com.

CPSIA information can be obtained
at www.ICGtesting.com
Printed in the USA
LVHW040627230323
742379LV00012BA/110